I Was the Woman at the Well

A Journey to Wholeness Through Well Living

"With joy you will draw water from the wells of salvation."
Isaiah 12:3

By Tassy Wofford

PublishAmerica
Baltimore

© 2007 by Tassy Wofford.
All rights reserved. No part of this book may be reproduced, stored in a retrieval system or transmitted in any form or by any means without the prior written permission of the publishers, except by a reviewer who may quote brief passages in a review to be printed in a newspaper, magazine or journal.

First printing

PublishAmerica has allowed this work to remain exactly as the author intended, verbatim, without editorial input.

Scripture taken from the HOLY BIBLE, NEW INTERNATIONAL VERSION. Copyright 1973, 1978, 1984 by International Bible Society. Used by permission of Zondervan Publishing House. All rights reserved.

Scripture quotations taken from AMPLIFIED BIBLE, Copyright 1954, 1958, 1962, 1964, 1965, 1987 by The Lockman Foundation. All rights reserved. Used by permission.

ISBN: 1-60441-541-X
PUBLISHED BY PUBLISHAMERICA, LLLP
www.publishamerica.com
Baltimore

Printed in the United States of America

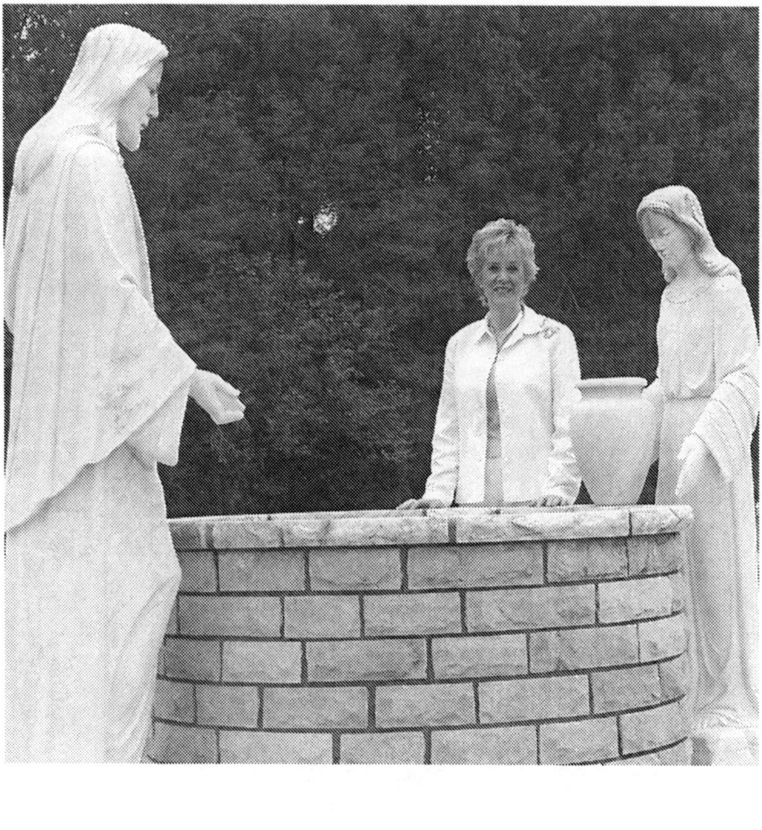

Dedication

This book is dedicated to the five most important people in my life. First, *Jehovah God*, my Heavenly Father, my "Abba"[1], the lover of my soul; *Jesus the Son*, my Savior, my Redeemer, my Husband and 'Well of Life'; and to the *Holy Spirit*, my Comforter, Counselor, Guide and Constant Companion. These three are responsible for giving me my *spiritual life* back and in more abundance than at its beginning. All the **GLORY** goes to them!!

AND

To my *Mother* and *Father*, they are responsible for giving me my *physical life*. I can now, finally, thank them for giving me my life without feeling deep regret, anger, and pain.

"When my father and my mother forsake me, then the LORD will take me up."
Psalm 27:10

Acknowledgments

"I appointed watchmen over you and said, 'Listen to the sound of the trumpet!'"
Jeremiah 6:17

The LORD has sent so many watchmen into my life to blow the trumpets of warning, encouragement and love. If I were to list all of my encouragers I fear it would fill up volumes. The heavy load I carried in my life long struggle of seeing any value in myself was lightened when He sent you to walk alongside me. I will be forever grateful for your input in my life and your belief in me—when I could not believe in myself!

Tiffany, my sweet daughter, if there is anything good that came out of my life it would have to be you! Thank you for putting up with my nonsense for thirty-four years! I want to say to you that I am sorry for all the pain I have caused you. I know I have not been the kind of mom you probably wanted and I was not there for you most of your life as you grew up. Emotionally I was not capable of loving you the way a mom should love a child and believe me I suffered from that inability more than you did! I truly understand what you feel and how you have suffered from the loss because I never had the unconditional love of a mother either! I wanted to be a better mom and show you more love but I just did not know how to. I am so proud of the beautiful young woman you have grown into and I give all the credit to the LORD, your loving dad and your grandmother Mildred. May the LORD restore to us the years the locust have eaten!

David Eagerton, my first 'Spiritual Father', thank you for teaching me the Word of God in my early years as a Christian and helping to build in me a strong foundation in His Word. Your enthusiasm for the Word of God made the Bible come alive to me and helped to develop my strong love for the Word of God. You gave me my first Bible in 1973 and though it is now falling apart, I still cherish it as one of my most precious possessions. A Bible that is falling apart is owned by a person who is not! You encouraged me in so many ways and left an imprint of Christ's love on my heart, thank you!

Fred Davies, Mr. Fred, you are the tender father figure the LORD placed in my life in 1972 to mentor and encourage me in so many ways, particularly in my art work. If I could have chosen an earthly father, you would be the one I would have chosen. Thanks for letting me adopt you; you were a rock for me when my feet were standing in slippery places. Ms. Lou, thank you for sharing your sweet husband and loving me too. You have always been the type of mother I would love to have called "mom". I love you both and words cannot express all you have done and been for me.

Pastor Phil Thrailkill, the best Pastor I have ever had! You showed me the unconditional love of the Savior. Thank you for not only being my Pastor but also for being a treasured friend! You are truly a tender loving shepherd for the sheep placed in your care. Thank you for loving me unconditionally and for seeing things in me that others never have, for noticing and appreciating the artistic flair in me. Thank you for your obedience to the LORD and coming by to visit me so many times when the Spirit bid you go. You were a 'rope of hope' to me many dark days when I was drowning in despair and pain. You always came by just when I needed a word of encouragement. Thank you Lori for being as supportive in your love for me as your husband is. Both of your presences in my life have been an indescribable blessing! My **hat** is off to you!

Kay Harris, my encouraging friend of thirty-one years. You are a trooper to hang in there with me for that long and still love me! Even though there have been periods of years we have not been in touch with each other, the love and friendship never ceased. Thank you for being my sounding board, my listening ear since the beginning days of writing this book. Thank you for believing that I should write this book and for encouraging me to **'write on'**. We have walked closely together these last three years during my healing journey and that has meant so much to me. God placed you close to me, even though we live two hours apart, to be a witness to the transformation of my life from hopelessness to joy. We have laughed, cried and loved together while watching the LORD'S miraculous work in my life. You were always there to share with me each precious gift the LORD sent my way. You told me that the LORD has used **me** to teach **you** about Him and His faithfulness but He has used **you** to show **me** true 'Christ like love' and that everything is going to be **"OK"**!

Kitty Dunn, you have been my best friend, sister, mother and confidant. Soul sisters and friends from the first day we met in 1985 at the law firm and travelers together on this hard road of life. Words cannot express to you enough thanks for the days you loved me when life was rotten and the times we laughed together when we wanted to cry. Thank you for all the days and nights you worried about my safety. You and Bob (who gave me away the last 2 times but I kept coming back!) have been there through the last of the three 'princes' of mine and watched me fall on my face time and again. Wait a minute that isn't fair, I have only seen you fall on your face once—**oh wait**, it was on your back not your face, in the rain forest in Maui! That priceless image will forever be etched in my mind and my first thought was—*"oh no, she's dead and how in the world am I going to carry her out of here"*! If you hadn't fallen on my camera we would have a photograph to remember the moment! I love you my friend, thanks for putting up with me and worrying about me all these years!

Mary Eastman, thank you for being Jesus' human hands of healing sent to me from the LORD. God has used your gift of healing to save my life and nurse me back to physical health from the first day I walked into the health store three years ago. You taught me how wonderful God's natural herbs are for the healing of our bodies and you must **never forget** that your obedience to God's call on your life is helping so many other people too! *Keep living your Dream!* Thank you for also being an encourager and giving your love in so many ways—especially in believing this book was supposed to be finished!

Thank you LORD for all the love you have sent my way!

Table of Contents

Introduction 13

Chapter 1: Foundational Truths 21
Chapter 2: The Fairy Tale Begins 40
Chapter 3: Search for the Prince Begins 59
Chapter 4: Prince Number 2 68
Chapter 5: Prince Number 3 87
Chapter 6: Prince Number 4 108
Chapter 7: Running from the Father 119
Chapter 8: The Last Straw 135
Chapter 9: Roses in the Wilderness 150
Chapter 10: Love Notes from My Father 173
Chapter 11: Happily Forever After 178
Chapter 12: The Journey Home 185

A Prayer for Salvation 189

About the Author 193

Notes 195

Introduction

"Listen, O daughter, consider and give ear; Forget your people and your father's house. The king is enthralled by your beauty; honor him, for he is your lord."
Psalm 45:10-11

Most of us grew up hearing and believing in the magical fairy tale stories about the 'Prince' who came to save the 'Damsel' in distress. These stories told us about a prince that rode in on his lofty white steed and rescued the beautiful damsel from the grip of the evil sorcerer who had her locked away in a tower. The two of them pledged their eternal undying love for one another and the story ended there with the phrase *"they lived happily ever after"*. Many like I, in our innocent trust as children, believed that our life would turn out just like these stories, we would be rescued by a handsome 'prince' and live "happily ever after". Unfortunately, these stories never told us the rest of the tale where the two of them went home to start housekeeping only to find out that neither one was perfect like the characters in the stories and neither of them could fill that empty hole inside that only God can fill.

This book is a modern day 'fairy tale' story based on the true-life story of a woman and her journey in search of her

'Prince Charming'. She was in search of the white knight who would ride into her life to rescue her and right all the wrongs and injustices that she had suffered. The man who could provide all of the affection, romance, tenderness, security, warmth and closeness she so desperately longed for all of her life but could not find. The man who could fill up all the empty places she had inside and quench the thirst she could not satisfy. She just wanted to find someone who would love her unconditionally, tell her how beautiful she was, and never walk out and leave her again. She needed that 'prince' to rescue her from the tower of pain that had become her home. She continued to search tirelessly in her journey for the intimacy and love that had eluded her from the earliest years of childhood into her numerous relationships and marriages. She wanted to find the fairy tale ending to the fairy tale beginning of her life but instead kept finding only nightmares! Then one day she found her 'Prince Charming' at a *'well'* and her life would never be the same! All of the other wells where she kept going to quench her insatiable thirst were always dry and barren but this *'well'* became her **fountain of life**. *"For with you is the fountain of life; in your light we see light."* (Psalm 36:9)

This is 'my life story' and it tells how I learned to live from the *'well of living water'*, **Jesus Christ**. It is a story about how God's wondrous love restored my hope and healed my brokenness! *"But whoever drinks the water I give him will never thirst. Indeed, the water I give him will become in him a spring of water welling up to eternal life."* (John 4:14) Please trust me when I say it has taken a lot of courage for me to obey the LORD'S direction to write this book and share many of the personal details of my life contained within these pages. However, it is my fervent prayer that my life story will become a beacon of hope for those of you who have lost your way in the darkness. I know there are many people out there living in the same kind of **'silent pain'** that I lived in for the greater part of my life due to my childhood losses. Somewhere along the way, most of our pulpits have failed to tell us that God not only wants to give us salvation through His son Jesus but He also wants to heal us and redeem our broken lives from the hand of the enemy. Jeremiah 31:16-17 says, *"'they will return from the land of the enemy. So there is hope for your future', declares the LORD."*

God in His sweet mercy and compassion has redeemed my life from the pit of despair and hopelessness that had become my permanent residence. I hope this book can be the **'rope of hope'** that God will use to pull you up out of whatever waterless well you may be living in today. Isaiah 42:22 describes so vividly the condition I believe many people are living in today, *"But this is a people plundered and looted, all of them trapped in pits or hidden away in prisons. They have become plunder, with no one to rescue them; they have been made loot, with no one to say, 'Send them back.'"* I have come to say, "Send them back to wholeness LORD, pull them up out of their pits and set them free from their prisons!"

My healing journey began one unforgettable day in 1999, as I drove past a cemetery I noticed a life-size statue of Jesus, by a well, talking with a woman. The statue captured my attention and seemed to haunt me each time I passed by. I could not get the image of the statue out of my mind. Then one day the Holy Spirit brought to my remembrance the story in the Gospel of John about Jesus and the Samaritan woman at the well. John 14:26 tells us that the Holy Spirit will teach us all things and bring all things to our remembrance. I had read the story before many times but this time there was **something different** about it; I could not get the story out of my spirit! Finally the Lord, through his Holy Spirit, led me to read the story of the 'woman at the well' again and revealed to me an amazing truth. John 16:13 tells us that the "Spirit of truth" will guide us into all truth and reveal to us whatever he hears from the Father. The Holy Spirit whispered to me in my spirit that day *"I WAS THAT WOMAN AT THE WELL"!* This startling revelation would only be the beginning of my healing journey to emotional wholeness. Four terrible years of rebellious running from the Lord would pass after this revelation before the real 'intensive care' healing processes started in September of 2004.

I want to share with you how I finally received the emotional healing I so desperately needed because of the lack of love and attention in my childhood. My story tells of the painful loss of my earthly father's love and the long journey home to find my Heavenly Father's sweet and tender love. It is a story of love about a man, a woman and a well filled with healing waters. The **'well'** I learned to live from that brought my healing is Jesus Christ and the water that quenched my thirst and changed my life so completely is the Word of God. I have found healing in the waters of God's eternal Word and have learned to live in it daily for my survival. Psalm 107:20 says, *"He sent forth his word and healed them; he rescued them from the grave."* Through my daily reading and searching in God's Word and crying out to God for His help, I found the healing I needed in my life, the healing that **nothing else** I tried had the power to do. The LORD healed me from my fears of never feeling safe or loved. Psalm 107:13 says, *"Then they cried to the LORD in their trouble, and he saved them from their distress."* The water that helped to heal me also represents the Holy Spirit, the very presence of Jesus living within us. John 14:16-17 tells us that Jesus will pray to the Father and He will send us a comforter that will abide with us and in us forever. Ephesians

5:26-27 tells us, *"to make her holy, cleansing her by the washing with water through the word, and to present her to himself as a radiant church, without stain or wrinkle or any other blemish, but holy and blameless."* When I look back to September of 2004, when God first placed me in the cocoon I have affectionately come to call **GICU** *"God's Intensive Care Unit"*, I stand in amazement of the transformation in me. The once lowly caterpillar is now free to soar like a beautiful butterfly on the wings of God's wind.

Within these pages is the story of how the sweet tenderness of our 'Great and Mighty God' loved me back to emotional and physical health. It tells how my Heavenly Father healed me from depression, fear of being alone and unloved, insecurity and so many other bondages. *"But I will restore you to health and heal your wounds, declares the LORD." (Jeremiah 30:17)* The Lord Jesus is a tender shepherd who guards and keeps His sheep with love and tenderness. Isaiah 40:11 says, *"He tends his flock like a shepherd: He gathers the lambs in his arms and carries them close to his heart."* I was one of the **stubborn sheep** that kept wandering off, trying to live on my own because of my brokenness from childhood. Because of Jesus' eternal love for me, He never gave up on His relentless pursuit to mend all of the broken places inside of me and teach me how much He truly loved me. In John 10:14 Jesus said that He was the good shepherd and that He would lay down His life for us. In John 10:28-30 Jesus also says, *"I give them eternal life, and they shall never perish; no one can snatch them out of my hand. My father, who has given them to me, is greater than all; no one can snatch them out of my Father's hand. I and the Father are one."*

My story is a journey that contains tragedy, abuse, loss, heartache, joy, healing, and triumph. You see, I lost my first

'Prince Charming', my daddy, when I was a very small child of three and I never knew what it was like to have someone love me unconditionally. I was determined to find another 'Prince' to fill his shoes, love me forever, and tell me how beautiful I was to him. I knew my 'Prince Charming' was out there and I needed to find him, so I set out on a journey to do just that. I was convinced that if I found him he would make everything in my life all right, he would **make me all right!** Fifty years and four husbands later, I finally found the only real 'Prince Charming', the 'Prince of Peace', Jesus the One and Only who can provide **ALL** that I will **ever** need!

My prayer for all of you that read this book is that it will lead you to the *'well of life'* that has taken me a lifetime of digging to find. My purpose is to give you hope for the emotional healing you may need. If I can triumph over my brokenness with God's help then there is hope for everyone! I know there are thousands of you out there, both women and men that are as thirsty as I was for a life with more meaning and filled with unconditional love. People just like me filled with such deep pain and hurt that some days you cannot even breathe. Many people we pass every day look like they are all together on the outside but on the inside they are screaming for help. I was one of those people until Jesus finally set me **FREE!** Everyone that I tell my story to makes the same profound comment, "but you look like you are so confident and have it all together". Oh, how far from the truth that statement was! I always made sure I looked perfect on the outside to try and disguise the mess on the inside! The only thing that is really at the heart of what each of us is searching for is—to LOVE and BE LOVED UNCONDITIONALLY forever! Jesus Christ is the only person that can truly accept, satisfy and love us unconditionally forever!!!

Come, go with me on this journey and meet this "Woman at the Well". As we lean over to gaze into this deep well and draw water, you may see your own reflection there and find the healing I have found. **Open your hearts and let the healing waters flow!**

"If anyone is thirsty, let him come to me and drink. Whoever believes in me, as the Scripture has said, streams of living water will flow from within him."
John 7:37-38

Chapter 1

Foundational Truths

"My people have committed two sins: They have forsaken me, the spring of living water, and have dug their own cisterns, broken cisterns that cannot hold water." (Jeremiah 2:13)

Every contractor knows that the foundation in any type of building is always critical. In order to withstand the weight of the building and other stresses that may come along, the foundation must be deep and solid. Our lives are like buildings, and the quality of their foundation will determine the quality of the whole. Far too often in both cases, inferior materials are used and when tests come, they both crumble. Such was the case in my life. Even though Jesus was my Savior, when the storms of life blew hard my faulty childhood foundation caused my walls to collapse. I had not allowed God to be my **sole** foundation and so I did not have enough strength to withstand the howling winds of life. *"He will be the sure foundation for your times, a rich store of salvation and wisdom and knowledge; the fear of the LORD is the key to this treasure."* (Isaiah 33:6)

Before we begin **'my journey'** to the **well of living waters**, I would like to introduce you to the story of the Samaritan woman at the well in the Gospel of John. Her story plays a pivotal role in the precious revelations and healings I have received from the Lord over the past several miles of my journey. The 'woman at the well' is primarily an important story about the salvation that Jesus offers us. There is however, a wealth of other hidden treasures in her story and the LORD used these truths in the healing of my brokenness. I want to share some of these treasures with you before I begin my life story of healing. God's Word has played a **major role** in my healing that has occurred over the last few years since 2004. *"He sent forth his word and healed them; he rescued them from the grave."* (Psalm 107:20) I have learned to draw the strength for my healing from this **'well of life'**. Psalm 119:92 says, *"If your law had not been my delight, I would have perished in my affliction."*

There is **healing life** in the Word of God. Jesus said in John 6:63, *"The spirit gives life; the flesh counts for nothing. The words I have spoken to you are spirit and they are life".* By living continually in the Word of God, I have found new life. In the story of the woman at the well, Jesus told her *"the water He gave would become a spring of water welling up to eternal life".* (John 4:14) In other words, Jesus was to become the **very essence** of survival for the believer's life.

Where there is water there is life for all things in creation, and where water is scarce, life has to struggle or just "throw in the towel." How many times have we all just wanted to "throw in the towel" and give up? Perhaps that is where you are now. Do not give up dear one, where there is Jesus there is always hope and life! I truly know this is true because in the year 2004 I was in the deepest and darkest pit of despair and hopelessness.

I was "past ready" to give up and throw in the towel. There is no pit so deep that his arms cannot reach down and pull you up and out. *"He brought me up also out of an horrible pit, out of the miry clay, and set my feet upon a rock, and established my goings."* (Psalm 40:2 KJV)

I was so defeated, hopeless and discouraged that I was just ready to give up and die! I was what you could call a "walking dead person"! Then my 'Prince Charming', Jesus Christ, rode to my rescue when He met me there at the *'well of living water'* in that cemetery, a place of the dead. I believe the Lord made a **very** profound statement about my life in the place He chose for His revelation to me. It spoke loudly of the condition of my life; I was literally 'the walking dead' and had become, as stone cold as the statues that would eventually be so instrumental in directing me to new life. The deep abiding love of God stepped in to resurrect me to a new life and planted a sweet song in my heart. He started healing my wounds and breaking off the chains of bondage that had bound and crippled me for so long. Oh, Praise His Holy name! Psalm 147:3 says, *"He heals the brokenhearted and binds up their wounds."* Today, as I write these words to you I am a woman full of joy, peace and hope. He has freed me from the chains of fear, depression and pain that so heavily weighed me down. Isaiah 61:11 says, *"He has sent me to bind up the brokenhearted, to proclaim freedom for the captives and release from darkness for the prisoners."* I can hardly believe that I am the same person and neither can most of my friends! I no longer have that loud screaming fear inside telling me I have to find a man so 'I can be happy and secure'! I have finally found the only man that can truly make me happy and complete and He is all I will ever need!

Many of you have probably read or heard the Samaritan

woman's story and others reading this may not have, so I would like to re-tell it for you below as a quick reference in our journey.

(John 4:4-19)

Now he had to go through Samaria. 4 So he came to a town in Samaria called Sychar, near the plot of ground Jacob had given to his son Joseph. 5 Jacob's well was there, and Jesus, tired as he was from the journey, sat down by the well. It was about the sixth hour. 6 When a Samaritan woman came to draw water, Jesus said to her, "Will you give me a drink?" 7 His disciples had gone into the town to buy food. 8 The Samaritan woman said to him, "You are a Jew and I am a Samaritan woman. How can you ask me for a drink?" For Jews do not associate with Samaritans. 9 Jesus answered her, "If you knew the gift of God and who it is that asks you for a drink, you would have asked him and he would have given you living water." 10 "Sir," the woman said, "you have nothing to draw with and the well is deep. Where can you get this living water? 11 Are you greater than our father Jacob, who gave us the well and drank from it himself, as did also his sons and flocks and herds?" 12 Jesus answered, "Everyone who drinks this water will be thirsty again, 13 but whoever drinks the water I give him will never thirst. Indeed, the water I give him will become in him a spring of water welling up to eternal life." 14 The woman said to him, "Sir, give me this water so that I won't get thirsty and have to keep coming here to draw water." 15 He told her, "Go, call your husband and come back." 16 "I have no husband," she replied. Jesus said to her, "You are right when you say you have no husband. 17 The fact is, you have had five husbands, and the man you now have is not your husband. What you have just said is quite true."18 "Sir," the woman said, "I can see that you are a prophet.19

(John 4:28-30)

Then, leaving her water jar, the woman went back to the town and said to the people,28 "Come, see a man who told me everything I ever did. Could this be the Christ?"29 They came out of the town and made their way toward him.30

(John 4:39-42)

Many of the Samaritans from that town believed in him because of the woman's testimony, "He told me everything I ever did."39 So when the Samaritans came to him, they urged him to stay with them, and he stayed two days.40 And because of his words many more became believers.41 They said to the woman, "We no longer believe just because of what you said; now we have heard for ourselves, and we know that this man really is the Savior of the world."42

Lessons About Wells

After the Lord brought me to the realization that **"*I was this woman at the well*"** and I picked myself up off the floor, He began to reveal to me many hidden nuggets of wisdom in her story that applied to my life. It took me a while to digest and accept this revelation about myself because I was living in denial about how my life had turned out. I blamed all of my failed relationships on everything but the real reason, **'*I was an emotional train wreck'*.** As I sit here writing this story today I can honestly say that I was "one of the most emotionally messed up people" you could ever know, *I just did not know it!* I thought everyone felt as messed up on the inside as I did! When I eventually accepted the truth the Lord showed me, He led me to do some research on wells and water and I found many interesting facts that would reveal to me some deeper hidden truths in this interesting story. I had never heard anyone else before teach many of these truths in this story. When we become born again believers through the prayer of salvation (Roman 10:9), the Holy Spirit comes to dwell within us permanently to teach and guide us into all truth. (John 14:26, 16:13) The Holy Spirit has been my teacher and guide through my healing process.

If we earnestly seek answers from the Lord, **we will find them**, (Jeremiah 29:13) and I was determined to find the answers I knew I needed to live the victorious spiritual life I kept hearing about but was not living myself. I was failing miserably in living my Christian life. Satan was becoming more victorious than I was and there was just something very wrong with that picture! This last round in the boxing ring with Satan had **severely** knocked me down and **almost out** and so I screamed out to Jesus "help me I'm going down and I cannot make it unless you fight this round for me". God's Word tells us in Exodus 15:3, *"the LORD is a warrior"*. *In Joshua 23:10(KJV) it says, "for the LORD your God, he it is who fighteth for you, as he hath promised."* I also knew God's Word said, *"We are more than conquerors through him who loved us"* (Romans 8:37) and so I cried out to the conqueror, my warrior and He heard me. Jesus said in Luke 11:9 KJV, *"And I say unto you, Ask, and it shall be given you; seek, and ye shall find; knock, and it shall be opened unto you"*. It is my hope that in sharing with you the truths I have found in my search for healing that they will help you in your search for the **"living**

waters you seek" that will quench your thirst for meaning and peace.

As I stated earlier, the most important part of this story in John is the salvation that it brings. In the very beginning words of the story, I found another incredibly beautiful part of this story that applies to everyone! In the NIV that I quoted above, it said, *"Now he had to go through Samaria."* (John 4:4). The King James translation of that same verse says, *"And he must needs go through Samaria".* Jesus "needed and/or had to go there" to offer his cleansing love and salvation to this hurting and sinful woman; and He would go out of His way to go there just for her. Oh precious ones, Jesus goes out of His way to seek out each one of us and bring us His cleansing love and salvation. *"For the Son of Man came to seek and to save what was lost."* (Luke 19:10) I have found in my life that not only did He seek me out when I was *first born again* but He has also gone out of His way **many** other times to find me when I *went astray*. Due to my emotional damage and resulting anger, I have wandered away many times and lived in my own sinful ways. Each time I returned to the Father, I have found amazing forgiveness in His eyes and compassion in His loving arms. Just like the story of the prodigal son, (Luke 15:11-20) the Father has always run to me, thrown His arms around me and showered me with kisses! Hosea 14:4 tells us *"I will heal their backsliding, I will love them freely; for mine anger is turned away from him."* (KJV)

To understand the great significance of the verse "go through Samaria" it is essential to understand some of the Jewish history of that day. The Samaritans were a mixed race between foreigners and Jews. They were impure in the opinion of full-blooded Jews who lived in the southern kingdom of Judah and thus the pure Jews hated this mixed race. They also felt that their fellow Jews who had intermarried had betrayed their people and nation. Thus, the Jews would not travel through Samaria and would *avoid them at any cost* because of this hatred and disapproval. They would rather travel hundreds of miles out of the way just to keep from having to go near these **unclean people!** No respectable Jewish man would ever even consider talking to this 'sinful Samaritan woman' much less seeking her out! None, that is, but Jesus! Oh let us forever praise Him for His great love for each of us and that He still goes out of His way to seek us out today—even in all our **sinful unclean ways!!!** No one is **too unclean** for Jesus to seek them out and offer them His cleansing love! Ezekiel 34:11 says, *"For this is what the Sovereign LORD says: I myself will search for my sheep and look after them."*

Jesus, being a full-blooded Jew from the royal line of David (according to Matthew 1:1-16), went there specifically to chose *"this Samaritan woman"*. Jesus does not look at our *race, color* or *anything else* about the outward man but only sees our hearts! In 1 Samuel 16:7 when the Lord tells Samuel to go and anoint King David He tells him *"for the LORD seeth not as man seeth; for man looketh on the outward appearance, but, the LORD looketh on the heart."* Oh Praise God, Jesus does not see us as others see us and **especially** the way we see ourselves! The obsession with my own outward appearance instead of my inner self had become a crippling load of bondage in my life. I felt like I had to look perfect all of the time to be acceptable or loveable. I am deeply concerned about the emphasis our culture places today on the outward appearance and little, if any, emphasis on the inner man. Advertisements bombard us today with the newest fashions, diets and plastic surgeries that can change the outer body. We never give a thought to the mess on the inside because no one sees that part of us! We can just cover all that up by fixing up the outside! I fell pray to this trap because of my low self worth. Jesus however sees our hearts and He wants to do some serious inner surgery on us! When we let Him fix the inside then the outside things just do not seem to matter that much anymore. We have gotten it all backwards though; we think if we change the *outside stuff* then the inside will feel better. It just does not work that way, trust me I know from experience!

Jesus had already seen the Samaritan woman's heart from afar. Jesus knew the love she was seeking and had not been able to find in any human man. He knew she needed this **"living water"** He was offering. The **"living water"** that would wash away all the sin and the pain in her life and provide her with the deep love she had been seeking all of her life! Oh, how precious you are Jesus! You choose us because you see our hearts from afar and then seek us out even in the midst of our worst sins before we ever see you coming! Luke 19:10 (KJV) says, *"For the Son of man is come to seek and save that which was lost."* Truly, I was a lost woman who loved the LORD but the chains of bondage were too heavy for me to live in victory.

The next nugget of wisdom I found pierced my heart like an arrow and began my healing process when I was finally able to let myself accept its truth! She no longer needed to go to the same well she had been going to, *'which was men'*, to quench that never-ending thirst inside of her. Jesus revealed this to her by the next statement He made to her. She said to him, *"Sir, give me this water so that I won't get thirsty and have to keep coming here to draw water".* (John 4:15) Jesus then told here to *"go, call your husband and come back"* (John 4:16). He was revealing to her where her **"here"** was that she was going in order to quench her thirst. It was to husbands/men just like me! My question then to you is **"Where is your here?"** If you are going to **anyone** or **anything** but Jesus, you will **never satisfy** your thirst and you will continue to go from well to well in your search. The staggering statistics concerning the vast number of people affected by depression and addictions seems to indicate an unquenchable thirst and emptiness definitely exists in our culture today.

Just like this woman at the well, I had also developed a cynical spirit toward all men due to my deep wounds and brokenness. I even thought to myself as I read the story, "now isn't that just like a man to change the subject when you ask him a question!" Folks, we are not just talking about any man for crying aloud, I was reading about Jesus, the Son of God! I was born again and filled with the Holy Spirit but, in my deep state of bondage at the time, I could not distinguish the difference! **"Men were men"**, I thought, and they all acted and treated a woman the same! I had been rejected so many times by the wrong men I allowed into my life that I lumped everyone in the same category, "harsh or unloving". I had received Jesus' salvation but I had not received His love because I did not think I deserved it!

All my life all I have ever wanted is for someone to love and accept me and yet I was not capable of accepting the most precious love of all, the love of Jesus because of my insecurity and low self-worth! *"How great is the love the Father has lavished on us, that we should be called children of God!"* (1 John 3:1) I knew in my head Jesus loved me because He died in my place but I was not able to accept that knowledge deep in my heart. I was not worth loving! I believe there are many of you out there that have not truly accepted His wondrous love either! In His statement to her, Jesus was not changing the subject, He was revealing to her where she was going to try to quench her inner thirst, where her **"here"** was! She was trying to fill that cavernous hole of emptiness in her life by finding a human man to love and accept her and tell her she was valuable. Like her, I too had tried **everyone** and **everything** because I could not trust the love Jesus was offering. As much as I needed unconditional love, I was incapable of accepting His love. I was in such bondage emotionally I wasn't capable of accepting or giving love, **even from Jesus**. Jesus was standing before her offering her the one thing she had really been seeking all her life, but probably had never experienced, ***unconditional love***! Here before this sinful woman stood, the first man that had ever looked at her with eyes of love and accepted her just the way she was. He knew about all her sin filled past and present yet still He was reaching out to her with overwhelming love and compassion. He told her everything she had ever done but His words did not hurt or make her feel condemned like the things everyone else always said about her. Jesus' words were coated in love and were spoken to bring her freedom not condemnation. Here was a man that knew her soul's deepest darkest secrets and somehow she was filled with joy not pain like before. Her soul found sweet release in His compassionate eyes of love. As much as she had always wanted that kind of love, she did not think she was worthy of it!

Let us just pause for a moment, use our imaginations, and speculate more about her life than we read in the Gospel story. Perhaps she had grown up without a father, he died when she was young or he had walked out on her and her mother. She may have lost both of her parents as a child and so she never received the kind of love she needed to grow up with a healthy self-esteem. Maybe she was a victim of physical or sexual abuse as a child. She may have married young only to have her husband be unfaithful or walk out on her. Maybe because she had low self-esteem she kept marrying, the same kind of abusive men she thought she deserved and so her pain kept growing deeper. Can you see yourself in any of these? Whatever the exact circumstances, the bottom line was she never received the nurturing unconditional love we all need as children to grow into healthy adults. She did not have a firm foundation built on solid rock but one built on sinking sand so, when the storms came and the winds blew she could not stand. Jesus told us in Matthew 7:24-27 that a man that builds his house on anything other than Him, the **solid rock**, will come crashing down.

Due to her deeply wounded emotions, she continued to make bad choices. She continued to pick the type of men that would abuse her and fulfill her belief about her own self-worth, that she just was not valuable. Why else would she have had five husbands and was now living with yet another man who was not her husband? She was addicted to men for her security just like I was. I had become a *"man-aholic"*!

Most wounded people make bad choices and marry other wounded people and then a pattern is established that continues. Until we get to the root of the wound, the pattern will not change but only continue and emotional healing cannot begin. Just like in a garden, we may pull up the weed but unless we dig it up from the root, it will just pop up again somewhere else and be even harder to pull up! It may even come back as more than one weed! If we ignore the weeds and the garden is not cultivated, the result can be disastrous. The unsightly weeds will continue to multiply until eventually they take over the whole garden, and choke out all of the beautiful flowers. The same thing can happen in our lives if we continue to ignore the wounds of our heart and not bring them to Jesus for healing. All of the beauty of the garden God has planted within us will become a barren wilderness. My life had become a barren wilderness, a desert place where nothing bloomed until God began to restore the garden of my life in 2004. *"I will plant in the wilderness the cedar, the acacia tree, and the myrtle, and the olive tree; I will set in the desert the fir tree, and the pine, and the box tree together, that they may see, and know, and consider, and understand together, that the hand of the LORD hath done this, and the Holy One of Israel hath created it."* Isaiah 41:19-20 (KJV)

Abused people, whether by physical, sexual or emotional abuse, are not able to love themselves and are unable to maintain healthy relationships of any kind. If you cannot love yourself, you are thus not able to give love to others. You cannot give away what you do not have! Until we realize and receive the **great love** God has for us we are not able to truly love others or ourselves. People who come from abuse or dysfunctional backgrounds are also not able to receive love from others because they do not believe they deserve love. As much as they want love, they reject love from others because they do not feel worthy of anyone's love. Because others have rejected them, they have also rejected themselves and do not believe they deserve anything good. Abused people also place unreasonable demands on the people they are in relationship with to give them what only God can give them, *unconditional love*. When their demands are unmet then they just change people, looking for someone else who can meet their unrealistic needs. They cannot see that the change really needs to occur in **them**! Due to the lack of nurturing love, attention and positive affirmation when I was a child, I was **deeply affected** in all of these ways. Most of my relationships were very unhealthy! God is the only one who can make the changes within us and I assure you from my experience HE REALLY CAN!

First God must reveal the problem to us when He feels we are ready to accept it and then He can begin to bring about the change in us if we are willing to ask for His help. Unfortunately, sometimes we need to come to the end of ourselves before we realize we need **His help!** God can then bring the problem out into His glorious light and show us the dark hidden things we do not even know exist within us. Daniel 2:22 says, *"He reveals deep and hidden things; he knows what lies in darkness, and light dwells with him."* This book is the story of how God made these changes in my life and in it; there is **hope for anyone** who is suffering as I was. Acts 10:34 tells us that, *"Of a truth I perceive that God is no respecter of persons"* and what the LORD Jesus has done for me He can do for you. In truth, I cannot stress it enough to you that I was one messed up woman! However, God is not finished with me yet even as I write this book. I am still a work in progress as we all are who belong to Jesus. But let me just say with great confidence—**"I've come a long way baby!"** Philippians 1:6 tells us that, *"being confident of this, that he who began a good work in you will carry it on to completion until the day of Christ Jesus."* I think some of us—like me—just take longer to get there because we fight God **every step of the way** in the process!

The Samaritan woman had also become a "marked woman" whose reputation grew larger with each new husband and live-in lover. Her insecurity and low self-esteem also grew ever bigger with each failure. The insecurity and shame she felt had spun a cocoon of protection around her heart that isolated her from the very intimacy with others that she so desperately needed. In those days, most people would have shunned her and that is why she was going to the well at midday so she would not have to suffer the looks of judgment and scorn from the other women. She just didn't fit in anywhere and she was already so insecure she couldn't handle any more rejection! However, she found acceptance in this man Jesus who could set her free from her cocoon to become the beautiful butterfly He created. In so many ways, my story is just like hers!

It may be hard for us today to understand the significance of the well and the part it played in ancient times because we just go to the faucet and turn it on to get our water. In Christ's day, as a rule, most peasant homes had no means of obtaining water but at the local well or spring. However, some advanced drainage and sewerage systems operated in later cities such as Caesarea and on the Temple site in Jerusalem but it was rare. The women normally would collect the water from the local well or spring at the beginning and end of every day. In most all cases, wells were located outside the city along the main road. They would collect the water in a large earthenware pitcher and carry it back to the home either on the shoulder or on their hip. The woman at the well had to walk possibly miles to get her water and then carry the heavy jar back home. How would you like to have lived back then? Personally, I am learning not to complain about walking a few steps to my washing machine to wash my clothes! In some parts of the world today, many people still live this way and don't have all the modern conveniences we have in America. We all need to learn to be more thankful for how blessed we are by God in our nation and start acknowledging once again that **He** is our provider and protector.

There were two types of wells used during the days Jesus lived, they were either spring-fed or a well in which water seeped in from rain and dew, collecting at the bottom. Because the collection of water was such a chore, everyone dreamed of the time when he would have his own cistern (a hole cut out of rock, rendered with waterproof plaster so that water could be stored in, and drawn from his own wellhead). At the end of the summer, the cistern was dry and it made a good hiding place.[2]

This is where I found the next nugget in the study of wells/cisterns. I had to ask myself what other wells or cisterns had I dug to hold the water essential for life that would quench my thirst? What other cistern was I hiding in for security? **How about you?** Is it your husband, children, career, money, possessions, drugs, alcohol or even your "religion"? Any place, other than Jesus Christ, where we try and hide is not a safe place if it isn't in Him! *"Woe to those who go down to Egypt for help, who rely on horses, who trust in the multitude of their chariots and in the great strength of their horsemen, but do not look to the Holy One of Israel, or seek help from the LORD."* (Isaiah 31:1)

Believe me I have tried most all of them but my main well source that I kept going to, like the 'woman at the well', was in men/husbands. Instead of five husbands like her, I have had only four! Something I am not particularly proud of you understand but that is where she and I both were going to try to fill up that thirst for real love, significance, security, satisfaction and a sense of belonging. *"I have dug wells in foreign lands and drunk the water there. With the soles of my feet I have dried up all the streams of Egypt."* (Isaiah 37:25) In my endless pursuit of the "water" I needed to quench my inner thirst you could probably say I have probably dried up all the streams not only in Egypt—but the entire world!

I challenge you as we journey together to take a good look at your life and see if the wells/cisterns you keep going to have been anything **other than Jesus**, the **"well of life"**. If you find this has been the case in your life, I assure you from my own personal experience, you will be **continually** digging new ones! The only well that never dries up and continually provides refreshing water is Jesus Christ and His eternal Word. He has rivers of living water that flow continually through Him from Heaven. Revelation 22:1 (KJV) says, *"And he showed me a pure river of water of life, clear as crystal, proceeding out of the throne of God and of the Lamb".*

According to Webster, *well* means *"to issue or pour forth"* and *issue* in its noun form means *"the act of sending out; publication; what is sent out; result; outcome."*[3] This is where I found my next nugget. After her encounter with Christ, the "woman at the well" became the very object where she had gone to seek her water—a well. John tells us she left her water jar and went back to town and told all the people to come and see a man who told her everything she had ever done (John 4:28-30, 39-42). She left her water jar at the well because now she was filled with the living water of Christ and she wasn't thirsty anymore! She didn't feel any condemnation from Jesus' words to her either but just deep relief because she felt the total acceptance He had for her that no one else had ever had. She 'went out' and 'began to pour forth' the good news of the *Messiah, the Christ, the anointed one.* She went away and shared with others the 'water of life' that had filled her well of thirst and set her free!

Also according to Webster, well in its definition to *'issue'* means *"emerge; and arise as a result or yield."*[4] The next nugget I discovered in this definition of well (to issue) was that the Samaritan woman *emerged* a new woman and *arose* to a new life because of her encounter with Jesus. She *yielded* to this new life within her. According to 2 Corinthians 5:17 (KJV), *"Therefore, if any man **be** in Christ, **he** is a new creation; old things have passed away; behold, all things are become new."* She probably went home and told her current lover that she was changing her life and he would have to move out! Maybe she even moved to another town far away so she could truly have a new start where no one knew her past but Jesus. Who knows, we can only speculate what this woman did after she met Jesus! It would take time as she followed Christ to tear down all those towering walls of hurt that had taken years to build. I can only say with certainty from my own life, because of my encounter with Jesus, there have been many changes in a different direction as I have continued to follow Him over the years. Some of the changes Christ has made in my life have been instant but most of them have taken time to tear down. Do I believe Jesus could have healed me instantly of all my emotional wounds? **Absolutely**, but because He has chosen to lead me down a longer path to healing I have gotten to know my **'Healer'** intimately instead of just my **'healing'**. I have come to know His faithfulness, love, tenderness, compassion and mercy in a way I would never have known through an instant healing process. I must admit that I have not always been eager to cooperate with the LORD in my healing process. Due to my growing anger and brokenness, I have run from the LORD many times. However, Jesus is helping me to tear down those towering walls of hurt that have crippled me for so long. Just like an onion, He has peeled off my chains of bondage one layer at a time as I was ready to cooperate with Him. Jesus is bringing me out of the darkness that I have lived in most of my life. Psalm 107:14 says, *"He brought them out of darkness and the deepest gloom and broke away their chains."* Oh, how I Praise His Holy name!

I also learned a lot about water in my research about wells. One of the main things I learned, that I had forgotten from Science 101, is that water is actually a **trinity**, made up of two molecules of hydrogen and one of oxygen that are magnetically attracted to one another. Now I found this very interesting especially since there is so much mention of water all throughout the Bible. **Hum**, a **trinity**—*just like the Father, Son* *and Holy Ghost*! (1 John 5:7) We know that no life on Earth can survive without the constant replenishment of water and we as believers cannot survive without the daily supply of the **"water of life"** Jesus Christ to sustain us either. In Revelation 21:6 Jesus said it all, *"He said to me: 'It is done. I am the Alpha and Omega, the beginning and the end. To him who is thirsty I will give to drink without cost from the spring of the water of life'."* It is up to us to go there to Jesus Christ alone, the **"well of living water"**, to satisfy our thirsts. *"Come, all you who are thirsty, come to the waters;"* (Isaiah 55:1)

We have briefly speculated on some of the exact details about the life of "the woman at the well" in John's Gospel. There is one thing I am sure of in the life of this woman from my own life experience; she no longer **walked in fear** with that loud, soul piercing cry inside that said, *"Just give me a man so I can be happy, I can't live without one"*! She had finally found her 'Prince' and as she would learn to cling fiercely to **Him and Him alone** with all her might, **He** would be **all** to her she would **ever need**! This 'Prince' would help her begin to rebuild her life, a life that had been ravaged by pain, into a life filled with unconditional love.

"They will rebuild the ancient ruins and restore the places long devastated; they will renew the ruined cities that have been devastated for generations."
(Isaiah 61:4)

Chapter 2

The Fairy Tale Begins

"A father to the fatherless, a defender of widows, is God in his holy dwelling."
Psalm 68:5

"*Once Upon a Time*" long ago in a far away land there lived a handsome 'Prince Charming' and the 'Princess' he loved. They met and fell in love and then a 'little princess' was born to them. OH, forgive me but I just had to start this chapter with those words because it seemed appropriate since I had been living in a **"fairy tale"** for most of my life looking for the 'Prince Charming' I lost as a little girl. The 'Prince' in my story, as I am sure you may have guessed by now was my father, the 'Princess' was my mother and of course the 'little princess' was me.

Most all little girls think of their fathers as a 'Prince', whether he is in reality or only in their imagined fantasy of him. Their father is the hero who can right all the wrongs and heal all the hurts they have. He heroically fights off all the dragons and evil sorcerers that come along to take her captive. He is the one who always protects and defends his 'little princess' and helps her to feel safe in his strong arms. The greatest thing a child can ever experience is *the love of a father*. The greatest loss a child can have is never to have known the safe unconditional love of a Godly father. Our concepts of our Heavenly Father usually come from the model of our earthly fathers. However, the sudden loss and absence of an earthly father in my life caused me to think of my Heavenly Father as distant and unconcerned about me. Most of what I know about an earthly father's love I have only imagined, read, or heard about. I was only to have that kind of earthly father's love for a short time before it was lost to me forever.

Nothing can rival the power of a father's love to restore, heal, mend and provide security. *Nothing* can make us feel safer than to curl up in the arms of our father, sitting in his big warm lap with our head resting safely on his bosom. A father is a safe harbor in the storms of life. Oh, how **deeply** my heart would cry out continually for this lost love for the major part of my life! Even as I pen these words, my heart still stops to yearn for my earthly father's tender arms to hold me and to feel his gentle kiss of fatherly love brush lightly across my forehead. A soft whisper of love saying, "I love you baby, you're so special to me". The loss of this kind of love would **unknowingly** govern all the decisions of my life, right and wrong, for years to come.

Due to the sudden loss of my father's love, the *resounding cry of fear* that it left within my soul would continue to scream loudly for someone to just make me **"feel safe and loved"**. Every failed relationship I experienced continued to turn up the volume of my insecurity. I realize now my Heavenly Father was always there watching over me from the day my earthly father died but I became too angry with him for "taking my daddy away" to acknowledge that He was my Father until just a few short years ago. Isaiah 46:3-4 describes so beautifully how the tender love of the LORD has cared for me throughout my life. It says, *"You whom I have upheld since your birth. Even to your old age and gray hairs I am he, I am he who will sustain you. I have made you and I will carry you; I will sustain you and I will rescue."* Jeremiah 49:11 also says, *"Leave your orphans; I will protect their lives"* and I can look back now and see where God was protecting me even when I was not aware of it or willing to acknowledge His protective care.

The hole that the loss of my father's love left in my heart was **huge**. It became the foundation stone for the fortress of insecurity that developed in my life. The lack of love, attention and positive affirmation from my mother continued to build the foundation layer of that fortress that would grow taller with every subsequent failure in my life. Because I never learned as a child deep down in the very core of my being that I was loved, wanted, special or worth protecting I developed a *severe inferiority complex*. My inferiority complex then produced in me shame, perfectionism, pride, negativism and a fear of everything. Instead of low self-esteem, I developed a severe case of **"no self-esteem"**.

Most of my knowledge of my earthy father comes from what others have told me about him. When I lost him in a car accident at the tender young age of three, I blotted out all my memories of him because of the dreadful pain, sense of loss and anger it left inside of me. I was too young to understand that the reason he did not return home that fateful Sunday was not that *he did not love me anymore* but because he had died and *could never come home again*. My mother was too devastated I think to sit down and explain what happened to my father. She was so overcome with her own grief she was unable to reach out to anyone. I am sure this scenario may be common to many of you.

Many small children today lose their fathers to death, divorce or maybe even just never knowing who they are. My prayer is that through sharing my story of loss it will help those of you who *need to find healing* for a similar loss of your own. I want to share with you there is hope to find that father's love no matter what age you are and introduce you to the tender love of a Heavenly Father that far surpasses any love we can find on this earth. Psalms 27:10 tells us, *"Though my father and mother forsake me, the LORD will receive me."* Truly, I can testify that He has received me with abundant love and continually wraps His loving arms around me every day!

I was told that my father was a very kind and gentle man. He was loved and respected by everyone and always willing to help anyone in need. My half sister Gail, who was seven when I was born, also loved him and said what a kind and gentle man he was. Since he was not my sister's natural father he always made sure he took up time with her so that she would feel loved and not left out. I know he was also handsome because I have a few photographs of him and some wonderful 8mm movies that he left behind. I did not find these movies he made until I was in my thirties but they are still a treasure to me to this day. I am so thankful my father loved photography because his pictures were the only images of him I would have to remember who he was. I can look at them and see the love and pride in his face as he held me in his arms. They still would not prove to be enough though to provide the reassurance of love I longed for.

My father lived in Miami Beach, Florida and owned a hotel on the beach called the Tatem Surf Club. It was a very popular place to stay back in the 1940's and 50's. On the rare occasions when my mother would talk about my father, she used to tell me the romantic story of how they met. My mother was divorced from her first husband and she lived in San Francisco,

California. She was invited by a girlfriend Eleanor Peterson to go to Miami for a vacation. They stayed at my father's hotel because Eleanor and her husband Pete were friends with my father. My mother was a fashion model for an exclusive department store in San Francisco at the time. She was a strikingly beautiful woman. She was what some people call a "show stopper". I can remember that whenever she walked into a room, people would always turn to look at her. My father fell in love with her instantly and every time she made reservations to return to California, he cancelled them. A month after they met my father asked her to marry him and my mother happily accepted. One month after they were married she became pregnant with me and let me just tell you—*I have been in a hurry ever since!*

My mother always described my father as being handsome with a golden tan and beautiful silver hair. She said he was a sharp dresser and was always "dressed to the nines". He always wore tailor made suites, especially white linen double breasted ones during the day and he would wear a tuxedo at night in the hotel. He was a true "Prince" in every sense of the word. They lived a life of luxury and glamour with yachts, big houses, racehorses, and all the material things they could ever want. There were always famous people like Lucille Ball, J. Edgar Hoover or Arthur Godfrey staying at my father's hotel. It was a true fairy tale story by the world's standards! A fairy tale story that I felt had been taken away from me so suddenly and never to return. My parents had everything but the one thing that gives life and significance, Jesus Christ. In Luke 12:23 Jesus said, *"The life is more than food, and the body is more than raiment."* In John 1:4 it also says that *"In him was life; and the life was the light of men."* The life *is Jesus* and sadly back then to my knowledge my parents did not know this giver of life.

One Sunday afternoon in 1956, my parent's world would come crashing down, never to be the same again. My daddy and mother went out for a Sunday drive to Palm Beach and a woman ran a stop sign, running their car into a telephone pole. My father burst his spleen on the steering wheel and after a week in the hospital, he died at the age of 51. I do not even know if my father is in Heaven today because I am not sure of his spiritual condition at the time of his death. Unless he knew Jesus Christ as his personal Savior and was born again my father did not go to Heaven. John 3:3 says, *"except a man be born again, he cannot see the kingdom of God"*.

My mother was only 32 and now she was a widow, single again with two small children. Physically my mother was not hurt badly, she just had stitches in her head, but emotionally I think his death crippled her for the rest of her life. My sister told me that after his funeral my mother disappeared for about a week and left us with the nanny. I guess she went away somewhere to grieve like a wounded animal that goes to a cave, hides, and licks his wounds to heal. I am sure I went to the funeral but I have no recollection of it. Counselors have told me that I just erased that part of my life from my memory because the pain was too hard to bear. It is amazing how one person's failure to stop at a sign can so tragically affect the lives of four other people—my father, mother, my sister and mine—forever.

My mother sold the hotel in Miami after my dad's death and we moved to Georgia where my father also owned a hotel. We used to go to the motel in Georgia and stay during the summer months to escape the heat in Miami. I grew up there in Statesboro, living at the motel until the fifth grade. Then, my mother sold the motel in Statesboro and we began to move around a lot. We lived in Georgia, California, and then returned to live in Savannah, Georgia in my junior high years. In my 9th grade year of high school, we moved back to Statesboro where we lived until I went to College there at Georgia Southern.

My childhood memories are not happy ones! My mother was already emotionally dysfunctional before my father's tragic death due to some type of abuse in her own childhood. She was not capable of providing me with the nurturing love that I needed as a child in order to grow into a healthy adult with a good self-image. I think she was very angry about the death of my father and that anger always manifested itself on my sister and me. In my grammar school years, she was gone a lot on trips. In my junior high school years, she partied and drank a lot. In my high school years, she lived most of the time in her bedroom watching television or reading. In reality I really grew up without a mother.

The discipline I received from my mother was not out of love but violent anger. She usually used a hairbrush or whatever she could put her hands on to beat us when we misbehaved. Once, when I was in high school she even used the heel of a shoe and beat me in the face until one of my eyes was blood red and closed shut for a week. I remember telling the kids at school that I was in an accident so they would not know what happened. She would lock me out of the house when she got mad at me and then scream at me if I went next door to our neighbors to spend the night. I was terrified of my own mother! I never really knew that was not normal until I married my first husband and he asked me why I was so afraid of my mother. When she called on the telephone, I would start trembling and he could see the fear in my face.

I cannot ever remember my mother holding me as a child and telling me how much she loved me. Her love for me was indifferent, I felt like I was just in her way. She was always telling me what was wrong with me instead of how proud of me she was. Oh, my plea to any parent reading this is that you realize how important it is to tell your children constantly how much you love them and how proud you are of them. Never tell them all of the things you see wrong with them but always tell them all of the good things about them. That was something I longed for desperately from my mother but she just wasn't capable of telling me. I did not understand her pain then and so I grew to have a love/hate relationship for my mother. I knew I was supposed to love her because she was my mother but I hated her too because she could not love me the way I needed her to love me.

All I can remember is my mother's anger and unhappiness. She had a violent temper and was always throwing things or screaming at us. I remember once sitting outside of the closed bedroom door and hearing my sister inside screaming, *"No mamma please don't cut my hair"*. She was punishing my sister, who was in high school at the time, by cutting off her beautiful hair. I remember being terrified wondering if I was next! She never spent any time with me. She was always going away somewhere but then she would bring back a present to make up to us for her absence. This pattern taught me that people buy your love to make up for their absence or bad behavior. This pattern was also repeated by two of the husbands I married. I did receive attention from my mother when I was sick so I was usually happy when I got sick because that meant she would spend a little time with me.

I played many hours by myself as a child and learned **"to be lonely"** from a very early age. I so desperately wanted someone to pay me some attention, to acknowledge my existence and take delight in me. The lack of healthy attention I needed as a child helped to build a terrible stronghold of insecurity in me. It followed me into adulthood and caused me to make **many** unhealthy relational choices just for the sake of having someone to pay me some **long overdue** attention.

The motel where we lived was out in the country so there were not a lot of children to play with. Occasionally a tourist with children would come to stay at the motel and that was usually a real treat for me. My sister was seven years older than I was and she was really more of a mother to me than a sister. She always looked after me when mom was gone. I can remember a couple of times when I accidentally broke something my sister actually stepped in front of me and took my beating for me. I guess in a strange kind of way back then my sister was my savior. She took the wrath I deserved from my mother.

My "sissy" Gail died in August of 2005 from the ravages of alcoholism at the age of 59. I found out she had died when I received court papers in the mail in February of 2007. Needless to say, I sat down on the floor in shock and cried in disbelief. No one had notified me of her death. The painful effects of our dysfunctional home had so crippled my sister that she lost her fight to live many years ago when she turned to comfort in alcohol. My sister lived in California and in 1999 at her children's request I went out there to try to help her. She had lived as a recluse in her house for many years just *drinking herself to death*. She was living like a "bag lady" in what was once a **very nice** six-figure house. We had to get the police to come and remove her from the house to take her to the hospital to get help. It was so devastating to me when I saw her appearance I could not even talk. I saw her last in 1988 at our mother's funeral and she was still a very beautiful woman. She was in her fifties in 1999 but she looked like a woman of 90! In just eleven years because of the alcohol and lack of physical care, she had aged forty years. Most of her teeth were gone and she was as thin as a rail, she looked like a skeleton! I just stood there and wept feeling a strong sense of "de ja vu" wash over me because of the striking physical and circumstantial resemblance to my mother.

I had watched my mother die exactly the same way about ten years before! They looked so much alike physically that it was like looking at my mother all over again. Even now I shudder as I think of how my sister looked when they brought her out of her house. I have watched both my mother and my sister waste their lives and die at early ages from the affects of alcoholism and I know that had the LORD not intervened in my life in 2004 I would have been the **next casualty**. They both ended up living in nursing homes at very young ages.

My mother died in 1988 at the age of 64 from the affects of alcohol, broken and unaware of anything or anyone around her. Some days when I went to visit her, she did not even know who I was. On the outside, they were both very beautiful women but on the inside lived only the dark shadows of twisted crippling pain. But for the grace of God, I would be in the same exact place!

When I was a small child I can remember my mother saying angry things to me like, "why don't you just go outside and play in the traffic" or "you should be glad that I even had you". Well, I was not glad! She was constantly telling me "I should be ashamed of myself" when I did something she thought was wrong and that remark really **sank down deep** within my spirit and remained there for *years to come.*

I spent many nights crying into my pillow asking God why He took my daddy and left me with such a hateful mother who did not want me. It says in Psalm 56:8 that God puts our tears in a bottle, well by the time I left adolescence He needed an Olympic swimming pool, and eventually would need an ocean to hold all of my tears! Oh I just wanted desperately to understand **if God loved me**, *how could He allow such an awful thing to happen to me?*

From my early childhood, I thought of God as an angry distant God just like the mother who was supposed to love me but didn't. We supposedly get our image of God from our earthly father who in my case was nonexistent because he died and left me. That left my mother in the place of my father and she was a very angry distant mother who did not want me. My concept of my heavenly Father thus developed into someone who was distant, cold, unloving, and angry with me most of the time. This idea imbedded itself so deeply in me that it has taken the LORD until this very day to show me that He is a loving God that only wants good things for me and not evil. *"For I know the plans I have for you, declares the LORD, 'plans to prosper you and not to harm you, plans to give you hope and a future'"*, Jeremiah 29:11. This is a lesson **He is still** in the process of teaching me today—*how very much He loves me!* I am sure I must be one of the **hardest** nuts He has ever had to crack in that department!

My mother also had a very critical spirit. She was constantly trying to change the way I looked and telling me I was too skinny. She told me my hair was too thin and she was always trying to get rid of my freckles with every new cream that came on the market. Her constant criticism destroyed any healthy self-esteem I should have developed as a child. I began to believe *the lie* that nothing about me was good on the inside or out. It is so extremely important to watch what we say to our children and to others. The words we speak can cripple and leave scars that take many years to heal. However, the soothing balm of the Lord Jesus' love can heal the scars that have been left. Ill spoken words can cause handicapped emotions that follow us well into adulthood. My warped perception of who I was caused me to make many bad decisions repeatedly! With each bad decision, my insecurity grew increasingly **deeper** and more **painful**. The deep need for love and acceptance led me into a string of bad marriages and relationships that nearly destroyed me.

In God's sovereignty when I was very small, He sent a Christian couple to care for my sister and me in my mother's absence. They provided some happy times and nurturing love that I could not get from her. Psalms 68:6 says that God sets the lonely in families and He surely did this for me even when I did not know Him personally as my Savior. I must have been three or four when they first came into my life. Mama Exie and Daddy Ralph was what I called them and they taught me many things that my mother did not. They lived near our hotel in a big farmhouse in the country with farm animals and fishponds. Mama Exie taught me the things a mother usually teaches you like sewing, needlework, and how to cook. Daddy Ralph seemed to enjoy spending time with me. He took me with him to feed the animals on the farm and he also took me fishing. We used to play music and dance together. It was great fun to laugh and be happy! They actually listened to me when I talked to them and it was wonderful! I felt like they genuinely loved and cared about me. This was something new to me! They provided the encouragement, positive affirmation and kindness that I so desperately needed!

I shudder to think how much more crippled I would have been if I had not had their loving influence in my life. It always seemed that just when I was happy with them and felt like a family, my mother would come home and it would end. My mother would get extremely jealous if I talked about them and the fun things we did. She would then say bad things about them to try to change my opinion of them. I guess in some strange way she was jealous of the love they gave me that she was unable to provide. I would then feel guilty for loving them and for being happy. All the good that had been done by them would unravel like a spool of yarn. The positive input I received from them was not enough however to override all of the negative things my mother said about me.

Daddy Ralph used to take me to his Baptist Church and I am sure that what I heard must have sunk into my spirit. God says in Isaiah 55:11, "...*my word shall not return to me void, but it shall accomplish that which I please, and it shall prosper in the thing whereto I sent it.*"

Mother did take us to church, Catholic, but back then the whole service was in Latin so you can imagine how much I got out of that experience! The only word I recognized was "Amen"! I went to First Communion and Confirmation classes but did not really understand what it all meant. I remember seeing the Stations of the Cross on the walls but I did not really understand the true meaning behind Jesus' death and resurrection. I just knew a nice man named Jesus died a terrible death on the cross and his mother's name was the Virgin Mary. After about the 6th grade we stopped going to church, which was fine with me because I never understood what they were saying anyway!

The only time that I remember being happy in my home was at Christmas. Mother always went *all out* in decorating at Christmas. We usually had so many presents we could not even get near the tree. She was happier during the holidays and even tried to show a little love toward us. Sadly, her happiness always passed as quickly as the holidays!

When my father died he left her fairly well off financially but she was not a good steward of the money he left. She never went to work after she sold all of the motels. She just continued to live the way she had lived with my father, buying whatever she wanted. So, by the time I reached junior high school the money was almost gone. It is a known fact that if you continue to take coal off the coal pile and do not replace it, eventually it disappears and that is just what happened to the money! However, she always made sure I was dressed well even if she had to charge clothes all over town! I learned from her that how you dressed and looked on the outside was **very** important. If you looked good on the outside everything was all right—even if the inside of you was a tangled up mess!! I also learned if you look good then people will like and accept you.

    I do not really know how we lived back then, I just know that by the time I was in high school she was extremely worried all the time. More than once, we had a knock on the door for repossession of the Cadillac! She did not answer the door; she pretended we were not home. She would then borrow money from somewhere and pay what was owed. We looked good and everything appeared fine to the world—even if we did not have a dime in the bank! Why she never went to work I do not know but as you can imagine watching her example did not teach me any work ethics or good monetary habits! I never learned that in order to eat, you work and I never learned how to manage money wisely either! One thing I did learn from my mother was how to lie my way out of a lot of things and I became pretty good at it!

    When the bad financial times came, many times my mother would say to me "I'll just kill myself and then you'll have plenty of money from the insurance and everything will be okay then". I interpreted that to say that when you cannot handle the trouble in life you just check out! Well that seed also planted itself deep into my garden of pain until one day it started springing forth during each season of hardship in my life. Satan would use this distorted way of thinking to try and destroy me in the years to come. However, God was faithful and because of my redemption through the blood of Jesus, He protected my life.

On the night before the Israelites were delivered out of Egypt, they were to apply the blood of a lamb to the doorposts of their houses so that the death angel would pass over them. This first Passover celebration was symbolic of Jesus' blood as "the Lamb of God" who takes away our sins and delivers us from the power of death. (John 1:36) Exodus 12:23 says, *"He will see the blood on the top and sides of the doorframe and will pass over that doorway, and he will not permit the destroyer to enter your houses and strike you down."* Jesus' blood was the blood of the "Passover Lamb" and it has protected my life many times from the destroyer (Satan).

My mother never remarried after my father's death but she did date occasionally and have some long term relationships. The many relationships with men I watched come and go in my mother's life helped to build the groundwork for unhealthy moral choices in my life also. She was not very discrete about her relationships and I guess I learned from her that sex out of marriage was okay. Yet, when I got to junior high school she constantly preached at me to be "good" and be careful around boys. I guess she was a victim of the "do as I say, not as I do" mentality!

I was not popular in high school and because peers can often be hurtful, they added to my low self-esteem as well. I thought that I was ugly and skinny and did not have a good personality and I am sure that manifested itself in the way I carried myself. The voices of my mother's disapproval had planted themselves deep inside. Nothing about me was good and I just needed someone to validate my worth, tell me I was beautiful and love me. I spent **a lot of time** at home alone drawing and sewing. I think I only had one boyfriend in high school that I can remember and so I very rarely had any dates. Life was terribly lonely for me and so I just lost myself in busyness painting or sewing. I watched old movies and spent a lot of time in my imagination thinking about the day a *wonderful prince* would ride into my life and rescue me from this tower of pain where I lived.

As I began to write about my childhood and life with my mother I came to the realization that my mother didn't teach me how to live, she taught me how to die. Even though there are so many negative things she did, my mother did also contribute some positive things. She had a tremendous talent for art but she never used it. I inherited this talent from her and I have tried to use it and not waste it as she did. She taught me grace, manners, flair for fashion and a wonderful sense of style. She was always immaculately and fashionably dressed and I inherited that flair from her also. I remember I used to love playing dress up in her beautiful clothes when I was a little girl. I would play for hours in her jewelry, hats and furs pretending that I was *a beautiful movie star or princess*. I still love to dress up in jewelry, hats and furs today!

Until recently I used to look at pictures of myself and think "oh how ugly I am", if I could only be as beautiful as my mother was. One day not too long ago, I was going through some family photos and came across a picture of myself from my early twenties. I thought to myself "wow I wasn't that ugly, in fact I was kind of pretty, my hair wasn't too thin, my freckles weren't ugly, and I had a beautiful smile". For the first time in my life I saw myself the way God sees me. Why had I come to think I looked so terrible? Because I had been criticized for so long, by so many people, that *I believed their lies* deep down inside.

I do not want to put all of the blame on my mother because there are many other people that I invited into my life over the past years that deepened this bondage of insecurity. She was just the springboard that launched me into a life of choosing others that reaffirmed my belief of worthlessness. However, oh, how great my Jesus is! He did not die to set me free from captivity for me to keep on living in bondage! Galatians 5:1 says, *"It is for freedom that Christ has set us free. Stand firm, then, and do not let yourselves be burdened again by a yoke of slavery."* He has started to heal me on the inside and show me that He thinks I am special. He is breaking off the chains that have held me captive in pain and fear for so long. Isaiah 43:4 says, *"Since you are precious and honored in my sight and because I love you, I will give men in exchange for you, and people in exchange for your life"*. God the Father gave us Jesus in exchange of a life of bondage to give us freedom and what a precious exchange it is!

I am only now in my mid fifties beginning to accept myself a little more as being valuable. I have always believed I had to look perfect and act perfect in order to receive love and acceptance. The chains of that bondage had become a very heavy load for me to carry. Jesus came to set the captives free and to release us from the bondage and pain of our past. Isaiah 52:2 says, *"Shake off your dust; rise up, sit enthroned, O Jerusalem. Free yourself from the chains on your neck, O captive Daughter of Zion."* I have lived too long underneath the dust and dirt of my past and I am ready to rise up and sit on the throne that is mine through Jesus' victory at the cross.

How about you, are you ready to be free of whatever chains are bound tightly around your neck? Isaiah 61:1 tells us that he has come *"to bind up the brokenhearted, proclaim freedom for the captives and release from darkness for the prisoners"*. If you are ready to be free then let me warn you, be prepared for a battle. Let me reassure you though from my experience it is definitely worth the fight to live in the freedom Christ died to give us. Satan wants to keeps us in chains because then we are no threat to his dark kingdom and we will not live in victory but continue in darkness. Jesus said in John 10:10, *"The thief comes only to steal and kill and destroy; I have come that they may have life; and have it to the full."* I want to live the full abundant life that Jesus died to give me, not just when I get to heaven but here and now on this earth. I can tell you from experience Satan has tried many times by my own hand to take my life but my God is faithful. Psalm 121: 7 says, *"The Lord will keep you from all harm—he will watch over your life; the Lord will watch over your coming and going both now and forever more."* We are not to be afraid of Satan because 1 John 4:4 says that the one that lives in us (Jesus) is greater than the one (Satan) that lives in the world.

By the time, I started college I was just ready to get away from my mother and all the unhappiness. I was so tired of coming home to a mother who was usually depressed, drinking or angry. She was always in her room by herself watching television or reading. Whenever she got mad at me, for even the least little thing, she would give me the "silent treatment" and not speak to me for 2 or 3 days at a time. As lonely, as that could be, sometimes I was glad because at least she was not yelling or saying mean things to me. Only on rare occasions did we watch television together, usually football games. We did not converse or interact very much at all. Her depression seemed to get worse when I was in high school and I think it was due to menopause, considering her age at the time. Back then in the sixties, the doctors usually prescribed valium to women with menopause and they only made her more depressed on top of the alcohol she drank. I did not understand then the pain that was causing her behavior but now I do and I can truly say I have forgiven her. She was a deeply wounded person and took that out on the people closest to her, which is what wounded people usually do. I am sure she loved me as much as she knew how but oh, what damage she caused! I was a mess! I was starved for love and attention! I guess you could say I was an accident waiting to happen by the time I went off to college. I was finally going off to look for that 'Prince' I had dreamed about—the one who would rescue me from the 'evil witch'!

"All the days ordained for me were written in your book before one of them came to be."
Psalm 139:16

Chapter 3

Search for the Prince Begins

"She will chase after her lovers but not catch them; she will look for them but not find them."
Hosea 2:7

I met my first 'prince' when I went to college. I went to the local college in Statesboro, Georgia where we were living. The first few months of college, I still lived at home with my mother. My mother eventually let me move into one of the dorms because she decided to go to California for a few months to live after my grandmother's death. My sister was living in San Francisco and California was really my mother's home and not the South.

In my first semester I received invitations to join some of the best sororities on campus and I was amazed because of my insecurity. I never belonged to any clubs in high school and so I was very excited. I didn't think anyone else wanted to spend time with me because after all my mother didn't want to. I was having a great time because there were always parties and functions to attend. I experienced a newfound freedom and I was making the best of it. I was making new friends and actually having a few dates, something that I was definitely not acquainted with. I thought I was an *ugly duckling* even though God saw me as a *swan*.

I had been in college about a year when I starting dating my future husband and the first 'prince'. As I said previously, I was not very experienced when it came to dating. I did not know much about sex either because that was a taboo subject—something my mother *never* talked about. I found out the hard way how you got pregnant and unbelievably I got pregnant the first time I had sex! When I realized I was pregnant I knew I could not have an abortion. Back then in the 1970's, abortions were not legal in my home state of Georgia but that was not the reason I did not want to get one. I knew some girls in the dorm that had gone to New York to get an abortion and I had seen the emotional pain that it caused them. I had enough pain already to deal with and I sure did not want to start adding more at this point. Even though I did not know the Lord at the time, I just knew deep in my heart that it was wrong to end the life of my baby. My reasoning was the baby was meant to be because I had gotten pregnant so easily so who was I to play God and end this life in me? Even though in many ways I was still a child, I wanted to have this baby so I could give it more love than I had received.

My boyfriend and I talked about what we should do and we decided we would get married. As I look back, I realize I was very fortunate that he was an honorable young man and was willing to marry me. Today, with the high rate of unwed young girls I suspect that is not the case anymore! Marriage is no longer honored as a sacred commitment anymore because the morals of our society have declined to such low depths that anything goes. Sex with anyone outside of marriage is not acceptable and correct according to God's Word and **He** still considers *marriage as sacred*. According to Hebrews 13:4, *"Marriage should be honored by all, and the marriage bed kept pure, for God will judge the adulterer and all the sexually immoral."*

    I went to meet his parents in Florence, South Carolina where they lived to tell them the news! Boy was I petrified! I just assumed that all parents were like my mother even though the parents of my girlfriends in high school were not mean. I asked God many times why he gave me such a messed up family life and not a loving one like my friends. His parents were very understanding and kind. They wanted to help us in any way they could. We discussed calmly what we should do and then we made the plans to get married. I told my sister over the telephone and made her tell my mother. *I was too scared to tell her!* Once again, my sister was my savior and told my mother the *happy news*.

    The fairy tale wedding that all little girls dream of was now out of the question! I would have to settle for just getting the 'prince' without all of the fanfare that went along with it. So, we quietly got married at the courthouse in a nearby town and then told everyone else that we had gotten married a month before we came home. You see, thirty years ago it would have been shocking to get pregnant before you were married. My how times have changed and not for the better I might add!

    I had now married my 'prince', the one who was going to *make everything all right*! He had rescued me from the "evil witch" that had me locked away in my prison of pain and now we would live happily ever after. Things would be just the way I had always read about and seen in the movies. *Not quite!* The fairy tale I had longed for turned into reality. The days of wine, roses and romance turned into nights of bottles and diapers. I had just turned 20 when Tiffany was born so I was really a baby having a baby especially in light of my immature emotional state. I had never been around babies and so I was clueless! His mother and sister helped show me how to take care of this tiny life that was depending on me for her survival. Survival—that was something I had not learned to do very well myself. God was gracious and had put me in a big family (Psalm 68:6) and they helped us a lot.

As you can guess my mother was none to happy about the news! She finally came to see me when Tiffany was about three months old. She was still so caught up in her own pain and dysfunctional life that I think I was the last thing on her mind. She had not been a loving nurturing mom so I did not expect her to be a loving grandmother, even though I wanted that so badly. I desperately needed her approval that *I* was a "good mom" but I did not receive that reassurance from her.

After Tiffany was born in October of 1972, I started going to Immanuel Baptist Church in Florence. God was already at work in my life even though I did not realize it. I believe when I was younger and I cried out to Him in my pain asking Him why He took my daddy and not my mother, God heard me and had already begun to reach out to me. Isaiah 65:1 says, *"I revealed myself to those who did not ask for me; I was found by those who did not seek me."* Because of God's great love for me, He reached down into this broken life and revealed to me the great gift of His Son. It was at Immanuel Church that the fullness of time had come for me to meet His Son Jesus. I gave my life to Jesus and accepted His gift of salvation and was baptized according to scripture. Acts 22:16 says, *"And now what are you waiting for? Get up, be baptized and wash your sins away, calling on his name".* God not only wanted to restore my relationship with Him I had lost because of sin but He also knew I was going to need the strength that only He could give me for the bumpy roads that lay ahead in my life. He knew that only His healing could stop the abuse and dysfunction that had been passed down by my mother.

Jesus was the real 'Prince' I had been looking for but unfortunately it would take me thirty more years to realize it! You see, I was able to receive the salvation Jesus offered but because of my deeply wounded heart and emotions, I was not able to receive His deep love for me. I loved Jesus for the sacrifice He made for me on the cross and was happy He had given me eternal life, but I did not understand the kind of love He wanted to give me even though I desperately needed it. John 3:16 tells us that God loved us so much He sent us His one and only Son to give us eternal life. Love to me equaled pain and as much as I needed love, I was also afraid of it. There was still some underlying anger in me directed at God and my father even though I would not realize it was there until years later.

My husband did not go to church with us much but I was very active. I took Tiffany often and I even taught a missions class for three year olds. I was learning, growing in the Lord, and as happy as someone with my wounded past could be. I had a wonderful Sunday school teacher who became a *spiritual father* to me. His teaching helped to build a foundation that would keep me cemented to the Lord and to God's Word through many difficult times ahead even when I would stray away on my own paths.

My first supernatural encounter with the Lord occurred in this church where I found the Lord Jesus, appropriately named Immanuel, 'God with Us'. Matthew 1:23 says, *"Behold, the virgin shall be with child, and shall bring forth a son, and they shall call his name Immanuel, which, being interpreted, is God with us."* I have had many supernatural signs and wonders given to me from the Lord over the years that have amazed me and I treasure them all in my heart. Deuteronomy 10:21 says, *"He is your praise; he is your God, who performed for you those great and awesome wonders you saw with your own eyes."*

On Christmas Eve, the same year that I was born again, my first realization that God was **"really with me"** occurred. *I will never forget it!* I had gone to candlelight service and was sitting with a girlfriend on the end of the back row. The lights in the church were dim and we were waiting for the service to begin. All of a sudden, I felt someone walk past us and stop directly behind me. I felt a light touch on my right shoulder and saw a slight shadow cast on my lap. Just as suddenly as they came, they were gone! I had an **indescribable** sense of peace and warmth wash all over me. I turned around immediately to see who it was so I could speak to them and there was *no one there.* I looked in both directions and there was no one walking away in either direction. My girlfriend then asked me who I was looking for and I told her what happened and asked her if she had seen anyone. She got the **strangest** look on her face and said that she had not seen anyone either. At that time, I thought that it had been an angel reassuring me of the protection surrounding me. One of my favorite verses at the time from Psalm 91:11 was, *"For he will command his angels concerning you to guard you in all your ways".* I came to realize later after many other similar encounters that it was the LORD himself reassuring me of His love and presence with me.

The years went by quickly and my 'prince' began to turn back into a frog because he did not stroke me with all the love and affection I desperately needed. My 'prince' could not fill up the empty places left in me in from childhood. He was a good man and a wonderful father to Tiffany but we did not have much in common and I did not know how to accept or give love. We did not have much of a social life either. We never went on vacations or did anything I thought was "fun" so I became disillusioned with this 'prince charming'! I was starving for attention because of my past lack of it and no human person could possibly give me what I needed to make me feel happy and fulfilled. I needed tons of affection and attention to validate my lack of self-worth that had grown so big.

We talked about counseling and so we did go to a supposedly "Christian" counselor for help. The reason I say supposedly "Christian" is because the advice he gave me was not based on scripture and I was too young in my walk with the Lord to understand that it should be. My husband only went a couple of times with me to counseling and then I continued to go by myself. I was much too impatient to wait on God to change this man into who I thought he should be! What I did not realize was that *I* needed a lot of changing! The counselor's advice to me was that we would be better off divorcing than for Tiffany to grown up in an unhappy quarrelling home. He told me just what I wanted to hear! There were no grounds for my divorce in God's eyes but in my eyes, he was not the right 'prince' and he just wasn't making me happy. Besides, I had to marry him, and so this marriage did not count in my opinion! In disobedience to God after seven years of marriage, I got a divorce. My husband came to me and asked me to stay and work it out but I was too stubborn to listen to anyone, even God! The fairy tale had ended once again and now I would have to search for a new 'prince'.

I moved out into an apartment and started looking for a job. I had never worked before and so going to work to support myself was a novel idea for me considering my family history! I thought life was hard when I was married but now the rough times really began. I had no previous work experience but I did finally find a job. Things were **very tough** financially because I was barely bringing home $80.00 a week and received only $100.00 a month for child support. Then I had an automobile accident and my car was totaled. I was not able to buy another car and so I lived without a car for three long years. It was a horrible time! In order to buy groceries I usually had to walk four blocks to the grocery store, take my groceries home in the cart and then return the cart to the store. I usually had to bum a ride *every where* I went! I found a wonderful woman that I worked with who gave me rides back and forth to work every day.

Right after I lost my car I had to ask Tiffany's dad to take her to school and bring her home in the afternoons when I got off from work.. I knew this could not continue and so I had to make one of the hardest decisions of my life. I decided to let Tiffany go and live with her daddy. I could not get her back and forth to school without a car and financially I was not able to buy another car at the time. Finances were very bad and I knew I did not want Tiffany to live the way I had lived with my mother and so I chose to give her a better life with her daddy. I knew he loved her very much and because he was a good daddy he would take very good care of her. The only way he would agree to the idea was if I would sign custody over to him. The day I signed the custody papers I remember sitting, staring at the papers and crying for what seemed like **hours** before I could finally sign them. I knew people were going to ridicule me for "giving away" my daughter but somehow I did not care. *I wanted what was best for her!* I knew in my heart that my decision to let her go live with her daddy took *a lot more love* on my part than selfishly keeping her with me just for appearance sake. I wanted her to be okay—*because I was not*—*and neither was life!*

I had failed again, this time as a mother and this failure threw me into a tailspin that would take me a **long time** to recover. I remember the day that her father came and got her furniture and clothes. I asked him to come while I was at work because I knew I could not stand to watch her things being moved. When I came home that night, I went into her room and I cannot **ever remember** a room being so **hauntingly empty**. I remember lying down on the floor in her room and sobbing myself to sleep only to awaken several hours later *alone once more*. Even though I was truly a born again person I had not considered what the LORD thought about my decision to get a divorce or paid attention to his commands. As a result, I was suffering the consequences of my decision. At the time I just wanted someone to make me happy and fill the emptiness and hunger I had inside for love and attention. Where was that **'wonderful prince'** that was supposed to make my fairy tale come true? Life had just not turned out **'happily ever after'** like the fairy tales I had read!

" 'The LORD will call you back as if you were a wife deserted and distressed in spirit—a wife who married young, only to be rejected,' says your God."
Isaiah 54:6

Chapter 4

Prince Number 2

"Do not put your trust in princes, in mortal men, who cannot save."
Psalm 146:3

My purpose in writing the chapters about the three other husbands that I have had is not to cast aspersions on them but to show how deep my desperation for love and attention had grown. I do not want to go into a lot of detail about each marriage but to just tell you enough to show how dysfunctional I had become before God started healing me in 2004. To show you the degree of abuse I was willing to suffer just so someone would love me! I also want to show how God in His love was still there for me in each marriage to protect and watch over me even though I did not think I needed His help. *"And behold, I am with you and will keep (watch over you with care, take notice of) you whoever you may go, and I will bring you back to this land; for I will not leave you until I have done all of which I have told you."* (Genesis 28:15 Amplified) The 'this land' represents a land of emotional wholeness that the LORD wanted to bring me into so that I could become all He created me to be from my birth. Each marriage was full of lots of pain, hurt, and abuse. So many cruel things took place that even now a wave of nausea sweeps over me as I remember the emotional pain I endured. It is hard now for me to comprehend how I could ever have imagined that I deserved the treatment I received. What I do want you to understand is that my husband number 2 and 3 were as wounded and dysfunctional as I was and that is why we were drawn to one another. I think their attraction to me was their need to control someone because they were out of control themselves on the inside. I was any easy target for them because I needed someone to control me since I was so out of control on the inside myself.

After the first divorce, the hunt was on once again to find my rescuer, the 'prince' who would rescue me from myself and wave his magical sword to make everything turn out right this time. In my growing anger at *God and myself,* I stopped going to church and started having fun doing my own thing. I started going out and partying and looking for another 'prince', the right one this time that would make me feel good about me again. I kept picking losers however, that treated me the way I thought I deserved, which was terrible! Each bad relationship deepened my insecurity and pain and so my choices grew steadily worse. It did not matter if they were younger, older, single or married. I just needed someone's attention and I did not care whom it came from or how I got it. I was growing so needy with each failure that no one who was healthy stayed around for very long. My deep neediness ran them away and the only ones I could hang on to for any length of time were dysfunctional people like me. This seems to be the pattern of a person with low self-esteem and I definitely fit the mold.

After three years in 1983 I finally bought another car, a $600.00 used Volkswagen and I was so happy. As you can imagine it was **very hard** to live without a car especially in our world today but somehow I managed to survive. I saw Tiffany on the weekends but that was extremely hard for me because every time she left I felt the **stabbing pain** of failure again. I would often make excuses not to see her because I just could not stand any more failure in my life. Every time she left, I would cry and be depressed for several days. I had failed on so many levels in my life and the pile was growing higher by leaps and bounds. I was in so much pain at the time that I did not see how much this was hurting my relationship with Tiffany. I was pushing her away to ease my pain, *just as my mother did with me*! Tiffany thought that I did not love her because I did not want to see her and spend time with her. She did not understand the pain I was in and I did not understand the scars my absence was leaving on her. *An exact pattern was being cut from the fabric of my own life with my mother.*

I believe that in God's sovereignty Tiffany turned out to be a better person by not living with me at the time because I was so dysfunctional. She had more family around her living with her daddy and the only family I had was a sister who lived 3,000 miles away. Living with her daddy, she had aunts, uncles, cousins and a grandmother that loved her dearly. Tiffany, along with all the other people that criticized me, did not understand that *it took a lot more love to give her up than to selfishly keep her with me.* The saddest part is that to this day, she and I still struggle with having a close relationship. My prayer is that God will heal that wound too and restore our lost years. Joel 2:25 says, *"I will repay you for the years the locusts have eaten."*

Well after three years of searching 'prince number two' finally waltzed into my life and swept me off my feet once again. I had dated many people but nothing lasted for very long. I met this new 'prince' through my place of employment. The relationship started with lots of attention from him and that is just what I needed because I was terribly lonely. He started bringing flowers and leaving them in my car along with sweet notes. Lots of wining and dining and gifts, the very thing I thought people who loved you did for you. He would come by and work on my Volkswagen when it needed fixing. I was really not attracted to him romantically but he was so attentive and please do remember I was **starved for attention**, even the wrong kind! I did not like being single, I just wanted someone to take care of me! I had always had an unexplainable fear deep down inside of me that kept screaming *"I was not going to make it, I couldn't take care of myself and I needed a man to feel safe"*.

We dated for six months and even though he was not a born again Christian we got married in November of 1983. I knew that I was not supposed to be unequally yoked with an unbeliever according to God's Word but I was living in a backslidden condition away from the LORD at the time and so I did not obey His commands once again. I would suffer the consequences of my disobedience for ten long years. 2 Corinthians 6:14 says, *"Do not be yoked together with unbelievers. For what do righteousness and wickedness have in common? Or what fellowship can light have with darkness?"* I had no idea at the time just how much darkness this marriage was going to bring into my life! The only thing we really had in common was insecurity and brokenness.

This was his first marriage and he had been living at home with his parents. He moved into my apartment and we lived there for the next six years until we were finally able to purchase a small house. He was 26 years old, five years younger than I was although he acted much older. He came from a large family and I really liked his mom and grandmother. They were so kind to me and they were also Christians. The day we got married, *at the courthouse again,* it poured rain like a **monsoon**. I remember someone telling me that if it rained on your wedding day it meant you would cry that many tears during your marriage. Well, I am not usually big on wives tales but I can tell you that saying had a lot of truth in it! I would cry that many tears and then some during the next ten years of that marriage.

Shortly after the wedding I felt like someone had flipped a light switch and turned him from a 'prince' into an 'evil toad'. I had married someone as insecure as myself (if not more) and I guess you could say it was like mixing dynamite with nitroglycerin. I truly believe that the screaming insecurity that I developed was largely due to this marriage. During this marriage, I lost what **little identity** I had developed after leaving my mother's control. The continual barrage of negative names and actions he directed toward me were devastating to my already small self-image. I started to believe all of the things he continuously said about me and even doubted my own sanity.

Now as I look back at his behavior he was very much like my mother in so many ways. He was very controlling and actually more verbally abusive than my mother. He had to be in control of everything I did, including how I dressed and who my friends were. He managed to whittle my friends down to only one by the time our marriage ended. That one friend, Kitty, was very dear and she managed to hang in there through all of his outbursts of mania. She is still a very dear friend to this day. After our divorce she shared with me that she spent many a night worried about me, afraid that I would not be alive the next morning after one of his fits of anger. I must confess to you that I spent many of those same nights thinking the same thing!

He had a volatile temper that would explode over the least little things. If I were, even ten minutes late coming home from work he would stand out on the sidewalk waiting for me and then yell at me when I got out of the car. He was also insanely jealous. If we ever went to the mall shopping and a male spoke to me, he would get angry and accuse me of having an affair with them or ask me if it was someone I had slept with before I met him. I finally got to the point that I did not want to go out anywhere for fear of running into someone that might speak to me and make him mad. I developed such a fear of his temper and yelling that whenever I heard him drive up in the driveway I would start shaking and wondering if I had done anything wrong that would cause him to be angry with me. Every time he would explode with anger and treat me terribly then he would always try to make up for it by buying me something pretty. Needless to say, by the time we divorced we had a house full of pretty things but not the one thing I wanted, **love and security**! It sounds eerily just like my fear of my mother and her behavior doesn't it?

There are far too many terrible incidences in this marriage for me to write about them all. My purpose in telling you about some of them and my life with this man is to show you how deeply troubled I was to put up with this kind of behavior. The reason I stayed in the marriage was because I was too afraid of failing again and I did not think I deserved better. I was afraid that no one else would want me if I got divorced again and I was afraid of being alone so I just resigned myself to endure the emotional abuse. Even now as I write about these things I cannot believe that I stayed in a marriage where there was so much cruelty. There were so many *cruel things* that were said and done to me it would take far too many pages to share them all. However, he never admitted that his behavior toward me was cruel or unreasonable because he was so dysfunctional himself.

One incident in particular occurred a couple of months after we got married that still makes me sick even now when I think about it! It makes me sick in the sense that I cannot believe I was so dysfunctional that I would have allowed it to happen. Before we married, I had a twelve-year-old blonde cocker spaniel named Brandy. He was my 'baby' and best friend. We had been through a lot of hard times together and he was always there to comfort and cry with me. Brandy was constantly lying by my feet or following me around wherever I went. My husband did not seem to mind my dog when we were dating but then after we married he started complaining all of the time about Brandy. He said he did not like dogs in the house and wanted me to give him away. We argued about it for several weeks. Then one day he told me he was taking Brandy to the pound and giving him away. I cried and pleaded with him but he put the leash on him anyway and out the door he went with me sitting on the stairs screaming and crying, 'no, please don't take him to the pound'. I cried and pleaded with him every night for a week begging him to go back and get Brandy. Finally, he went back, got him, and brought him home. Brandy was ecstatic when he saw me. My dog was sick and throwing up from all of the ticks and fleas that had gotten on him at the pound. I bathed him, pulled all of the ticks off him and he curled up next to me and went to sleep. Several days later, my husband told me Brandy had run out the door and away from him when he went by the apartment to pick up something. Brandy had never done that before! Whenever I let him out to go to the bathroom he always stayed very close to the apartment. When I came home, Brandy still was nowhere in sight and I knew something was wrong. I started crying and decided I was going to look for him because it was getting dark outside. My husband would not let me go and he said he would go find my dog. Well, he came home about thirty minutes later and told me he found him on the side of the road and a car had hit him. I remember screaming and going and sitting down on the floor and sobbing. He told me Brandy was in the trunk of his car and he was going to go and bury him. He would not let me go out and see his body. I don't think Brandy was really in the trunk of the car! I believe he simply did not want the dog around and he got rid of him by telling me he was dead! There would be no going back again to get him if I thought Brandy was dead. I was too afraid of him to prevent his giving my dog away in the first place or to go outside to see for myself if he was really dead. I think I believed his story in the beginning because after all, he was my husband and *surely*—he would not have lied and done something so deceptive.

As the years went by, I changed my thinking about the truthfulness of his story! To this day, I believe he took Brandy back to the pound and just lied to me about his being hit by a car. I will probably never know what really happened to my sweet puppy. I am sorry Brandy for not being able to stand up for you better. It still brings tears to my eyes when I think about what might have happened to him. *Oh, how could someone be that cruel, especially to his own wife?*

Many other things happened right after we were married that sent up red flags but I still stayed in the marriage because I did not want to be alone again. The constant verbal and emotional abuse I suffered caused me to build up a very high wall of protection from him. After a while, I did not want anything to do with him sexually or in any other way. I just wanted to protect myself from his outbursts of anger and hostility. During the last couple of years of our marriage, we were just two people living as roommates in the same house enduring one another's presence. Eventually, a younger girl came along that showed him the sexual attention he needed to build his own low self-esteem. I was no longer able to give him the sexual attention he needed because of the years of emotional abuse. It was hard for me to be intimate with a man who could say the things he said to me. He had an affair with this girl thus ending our marriage of ten years. It ended in a very ugly way with him trying to make me hate him to make himself feel better about what he was doing to me. The irony in it all was that he ended up doing the very thing he continually accused me of during our marriage, *being unfaithful*. I still have to wonder if she was the first affair he ever had because usually people accuse you of the very thing they are doing themselves!

The LORD is so tender and loving towards those He has made. God started working in my life in little ways to draw me back to Him about a year and a half before our divorce. He knew I would need **His strength** to get through the trials that lay ahead of me. *"God is our refuge and strength, an ever-present help in trouble. Therefore we will not fear, though the earth give way and the mountains fall into the heart of the sea, though its waters roar and foam and the mountains quake with their surging."* (Psalm 46:1-2) I had become so miserable in this marriage that I was actually becoming physically sick and I just wanted to die. I went to the doctor for tests but they did not show anything physically wrong with me. I was actually spiritually sick because I was living in rebellion to the LORD and it was making miserable inside.

I had not been sleeping much at night until one night in March the Lord came to my room to reassure and remind me of **HIS presence with me**. My husband was already asleep and I had been lying there for some time trying to fall asleep. Suddenly the room filled with the strong smell of sweet perfume. I must have been sniffing rather loudly while trying to figure out if it was really there because my husband woke up and asked me what in the #*#* was I doing. I asked him "don't you smell that perfume"? He answered rather gruffly "what perfume" and told me to be quiet and go to sleep. Well, I knew it was there because I could smell it so strongly and it reminded me of a perfume my grandmother used to wear. All of a sudden I felt someone's presence beside me. I couldn't see anything because it was dark in the room but I knew someone was there. I decided to reach out and try to touch whoever it was and as soon as I did a feeling of warmth started in my fingertips, continued up my arm and then spread throughout my whole body. I felt as if a bright light had lit the entire room even though in reality it was still very dark. Then an incredible peace washed over me that I had never experienced in my life and quietly in my spirit I heard the words, *"I am here, I have always been here with you and everything is going to be alright"*. With a wonderful sense of awe and wonder I then fell asleep and slept sounder than I had slept in years.

The next morning I awoke wondering *"who was that in my room?"* I even wondered was it a dream or did it really happen? Had it been my grandmother or an angel sent to comfort me? I began to pray and ask the Lord to reveal the answer to me. I started going back to church several weeks later and I found my answer one Sunday morning in the words of a song named "He's Alive". This song tells about Peter and his denial of the Lord Jesus during His darkest hour. (John 18:17-27) Then after Jesus' resurrection, Peter was feeling terrible about his denial and suddenly the Lord Jesus appeared in his room. The song said—suddenly the room filled with sweet perfume and there before him bathed in brilliant light stood the Lord Jesus telling him "you are forgiven and heaven's gates are open wide". I knew then that it was the Lord Jesus in my room comforting me in my darkest hour and telling me *I was not alone, He was with me and everything was going to be alright.*

    I just recently found out that the fragrance I thought was my grandmother's perfume was actually frankincense and myrrh, the spices they used to prepare bodies for burial in the time of Jesus. John 19:39-40 says, *"Nicodemus brought a mixture of myrrh and aloes, about seventy-five pounds. Taking Jesus' body, the two of them wrapped it, with the spices, in strips of linen. This was in accordance with Jewish customs."* I had always been curious about the fragrance in my room that night so I asked a friend of mine to mix up frankincense and myrrh for me to smell. As soon as I smelled it, I felt cold chills run up and down my spine and the hair on the back of my neck stood on end. I knew immediately that was the smell in my room that night, there was no mistaking its sweet fragrance. *"All your robes are fragrant with myrrh and aloes and cassia; from palaces adorned with ivory the music of the strings makes you glad."* (Psalm 45:8) Jesus had indeed come to me in my darkest hour to fill it with His glorious light. He came to pour the fragrance of His sweet perfume on the wounds of my heart and calm the storm that raged around me. He came to fill me with **His perfect peace**. To speak words of hope to one who had lost all hope in life. To tell me He was there and I was not alone. He tells us in His Word, *"Never will I leave you; never will I forsake you."* (Hebrews 13:5) I believe that when we see Jesus in Heaven that **sweet fragrance** will still surround Him to **always remind us** of His death, burial and resurrection **on our behalf**.

    Several months after my experience with the perfume, the Lord touched my life again in another amazing way. I was cooking dinner one night and I began to cry uncontrollably. My marriage was starting to come apart at the seams by now. As I look back, I believe the unfaithfulness had already started even though I was completely oblivious to it. I knew his behavior was very strange and I did not understand what was going on. He was doing things he never did before and all the signs pointed to an affair but I just did not know to look for them. That was the farthest thing from my mind that he was capable of doing after all the **HELL** he had put me through with his jealous tirades. He got mad at me because I could not stop crying and so he stormed out of the house and left.

After my husband left I stopped cooking, went into the bedroom, and dropped to my knees in despair. I began to cry aloud to the Lord and tell Him that I needed Him, I could not go on any further and He heard me. Even though I was in disobedience, I still belonged to God because of the death of Jesus on my behalf. I gave control of my life back to Him that night and asked Him to please help me. I asked Him to forgive me of all my sins in the past and present (there were a lot of them) and told Him I was sorry for my disobedience. All of a sudden, I felt like someone opened up the top of my head and a crystal clear river of water washed all the way through me cleansing me completely. *"He that believeth on me, as the scripture hath said, out of his heart shall flow rivers of living water."* (John 7:38 KJV) I knew I had been cleansed of all my past sins because I felt cleaner inside than I had ever felt before in my life. 1 John 1:9 tells us, *"If we confess our sins, he is faithful and just to forgive us our sins, and to cleanse us from all unrighteousness."*

It was truly an amazing experience! I know that everyone does not have the kind of experiences that I have had with God and I don't presume to know why God has chosen to give them to me but I thank Him for them. All I know is that I desperately needed Jesus' help and loved Him with all my heart and He chose to bless me in this special way.

My purpose in sharing many of these amazing experiences is to show you that even though I was a terrible mess God *had not given up on me or abandoned me.* He will never give up or abandon you either! There is no pit too deep that **HE** cannot lift you out of it. By showing you the condition of my troubled soul, it also shows you the wonder of God's mercy and healing. Nehemiah 9:31 says, *"But in your great mercy you did not put an end to them or abandon them, for you are a gracious and merciful God."* Even though I was still angry with God about my father's death, God had not forgotten me or let me go! He never abandons His children! I did still read my Bible and pray. I had not forgotten God or stopped loving Him; I had just put Him on the back shelf for a while until I needed Him. I wanted to be in control of my life because I thought He had let me down when He let my father die. The amazing part is that in spite of my rebelliousness and anger toward Him Jesus came to draw me back to Him before I ever knew how desperately I was going to need Him in the next year. Just like the Samaritan woman, He sought me out once again and *it would not be the last time*!

We got divorced on the grounds of adultery, which is what he wanted. He wanted to be free as soon as possible to marry her and the grounds of adultery only took three months to finalize a divorce. I was willing to forgive him and even begged him to let's try to work it out by going to counseling. He wanted no part of counseling. He told me he knew his responsibility was with me but he wanted to marry her. I was shattered to the core because of the rejection I felt. I did not want to be divorced again either. Even though it would be a release from an unhappy marriage for me, I did not want a divorce because it meant I would be alone again. I just did not know who I was and what I was supposed to do with myself now. I was alone again and in such pain, *I could hardly breathe!* I was brokenhearted by the betrayal even though it had been an unhappy marriage and my spirit was crushed. Psalm 34:18 says, *"The LORD is close to the brokenhearted and saves those who are crushed in spirit."*

As I cried out to the LORD for help He heard me and comforted my pain in a way that I cannot explain. He truly brought me the peace that **"passeth all understanding"** according to Philippians 4:7. There are so many verses from God's Word that became life lines for me in those days but one in particular was Jeremiah 29:11-13. It says, *"For I know the plans I have for you declares the LORD, 'plans to prosper you and not to harm you, plans to give you hope and a future. Then you will call upon me and come and pray to me, and I will listen to you. You will seek me and find me when you seek me with all your heart. I will be found by you,' declares the LORD, 'and will bring you back from captivity".* I used to focus more on the first part of the verses that talked about giving me *'a hope and a future'* than the last part of the verses. I can tell you though that now the last part of the promise has come to pass. In 2004, when I started seeking Him with all my heart I found Him and now He is bringing me out of captivity and into the Promised Land. Jeremiah 31:9 describes perfectly what God has done in my life, *"They will come with weeping; they will pray as I bring them back. I will lead them beside streams of water on a level path where they will not stumble."*

Several days after he moved out of our house I thought about suicide for the first time because I did not want to start over and be alone again. I sat on the bed and I took the .380 revolver out of the drawer and began to turn the cylinder. I decided I would try to pull the trigger and see how hard it would be to pull. I had taken all of the bullets out except one and thought I had moved an empty cylinder in line to fire next but I had not. When I pointed the gun toward the closet door and pulled the trigger the gun fired and **scared me to death**. Sadly, my first thought was how mad he would be if I had blown a hole in the wall or door and not that I had just been considering ending my own life. There were very powerful bullets in the gun and it should have made a big hole in whatever it hit. I sat dazed for a minute and then when I pulled myself together I got up to see what the bullet had hit. I knew there had to be a hole in something wherever the bullet had entered. I had heard the strangest sound like a loud metal ping noise after I pulled the trigger. It sounded almost like the bullet had been caught in a metal bucket or something. I looked everywhere and there was **no hole in anything** and **no sign of the bullet**! I know that the gun had fired because there was an empty shell in the cylinder and I could smell the powder. Even when I eventually moved out of the house I looked again to see if there was any sign of a bullet hole and there was none! I truly believe that the LORD had sent an angel to catch that bullet and protect me from any harm. Psalm 34:7 says, *"The angel of the LORD encamps around those who fear him, and he delivers them."* I am sad to say that over the next few years I would keep that angel **busy** protecting my life that I was so eager to end. Thank you Father, for never giving up on me! *"A righteous man may have many troubles, but the LORD delivers him from them all."* (Psalm 34:19)

Before we divorced I had grown close to the LORD and was always reading His Word. I was very active in my church and so I had a support system of believers to help me through this painful experience but I still felt so alone and frightened. I also was embarrassed because so many people knew about his adultery and I felt very **rejected** and **undesirable**. I read the Bible for comfort, especially the Psalms and some nights I hurt so badly that all I could do was hug my Bible and go to sleep holding it in my arms. I did not understand why this had all happened and why I had to be ALONE again. It never occurred to me that because of my dysfunction I had made another bad marriage choice.

Miraculously I was able to forgive him of the adultery and all the pain he caused me. I say it was a miracle because I know that the only way I was able to do this was by the power of Christ that lives in me. The pain inside was great and I knew that the only way I would survive it was through God's power so I cried out for His help and He heard me. *"The eyes of the LORD are on the righteous and his ears are attentive to their cry"* (Psalm 34:15) In my times of prayer and crying out to Him, the LORD showed me that in order for me to overcome the bitterness and devastation I felt I would have to forgive my ex-husband. Unless I determined not to embrace the bitterness and let it go in forgiveness, it would cripple me as long as I held on to it. I asked the LORD, *"How can I forgive him after all he has done to me"?* He answered me quietly in my heart and I fell to the floor on my face in humility. The LORD said to me, *"If I can forgive you of all that you have done then how can you do any less for him"?* I knew that this word was straight from my Savior and I must obey but I needed his power in order to forgive him. *"For the word of the LORD is right and true; he is faithful in all he does."* (Psalm 33:4) He had indeed forgiven me for many sins and I knew the sacrifice it cost Him, the precious blood of His son Jesus. Isaiah 43:25 says so beautifully, *"I, even I, am he who blots out your transgressions, for my own sake, and remembers your sins no more."* Thank you sweet Jesus for your precious sacrifice that brought my forgiveness!

My recovery from the bitterness and pain of the betrayal was so great that I was even able to eventually remain friends with my ex-husband. By the grace of God I was able to be there to comfort and listen to him when the same woman divorced him for another man just a short time after their marriage. Many of my friends (even Christians) did not understand how I could even talk with him much less offer him sympathy and I told them exactly what the LORD had told me, "if the LORD can forgive me of all my sins how can I do any less to anyone else". I had been comforted by the LORD in my great pain and so I was able to comfort someone else in their pain, even the very one who had caused mine! Praise God, only **He** is able to do this kind of healing **if** we cry out for His help. 2 Corinthians 1:3-4 says it all, *"Praise be to the God and Father of our Lord Jesus Christ, the Father of compassion and the God of all comfort, who comforts us in all our troubles, so that we can comfort those in any trouble with the comfort we ourselves have received from God."*

I know that my forgiveness of him had a great impact on him too. As I stated earlier he was not a Christian when we married. He was very bitter toward Christianity because of something in his past and so when I rededicated my life to Jesus and started going back to Church he became angry and gave me a really hard time. After we divorced and I was compassionate and forgiving to him he told me that he did not understand how I could be so nice to him after all he had done to me. I told him that it was **not** in my power to do it but that it was **Christ** that lived in me that enabled me to forgive him and be kind to him because Jesus had forgiven me so much. He said that I was the only Christian he had known that was actually living what they professed and that maybe there was some truth to the Christian life. Trust me when I say I have not always lived it by the book and I have failed many times but I do know that when we live it the way Jesus did in **"His power"** we can have an impact on the people around us! That is the only way we can bring people to the Christ who saves us from sin and ourselves! Not in our strength but **His**! *"But when the multitudes saw it, they marveled, and glorified God, who had given such power unto men."* (Matthew 9:8 KJV)

After the divorce, I had to sell the house we lived in because I could not afford the upkeep on it. It was an older house and needed to have some work done on it so I put if up for sale and rented a townhouse apartment. I also had to auction over half of our antique furniture because I did not have enough room in the apartment for everything. That was something that I really did not want to do. I felt like Job! I lost my husband, house, furniture, sense of identity and *my mind* all in one swipe!

I had been at home painting portraits for a living before the divorce but I was not making a lot of money at the time. A couple of years before our divorce I had quit legal secretarial work to stay home and paint portraits full time. I had continued to work full time during most of our marriage because his income alone was not enough to support us. My art business was just beginning to flourish when we divorced. I did not want to go back to an office and work because I was so miserable when I was not painting. I had gotten myself into a lot of debt with credit cards however because shopping was one of the **other ways** I used to try to satisfy the emptiness I felt inside. It always felt great when I bought something new but that feeling did not last very long and when the bills came I felt **even worse**! It is a vicious cycle that can suck you in and take you down into a bottomless pit of debt. So, selling the house seemed like the logical answer to my problems. I took the little bit of profit I made from the sale of the house and paid off some of the bills but it only paid off about half of the debt.

God has blessed me with a tremendous natural talent in art but unlike my mother I promised to use it. I actually do have to thank my second husband for the encouragement he gave me concerning my art talent. He was always buying me art supplies and telling me to experiment with new mediums until I finally found my gift in painting portraits. He is the one that pushed me to pursue and develop my art into what it is today. I guess there was some good that came out of that bad marriage!

Eventually I began to start my life over again with the help of the LORD and tried to put the pieces back together and the pain behind me. In many ways, the death of this marriage would bring new life and was actually an escape from the misery I was living in. God rescued me out of the stormy marriage filled with verbal and emotional abuse and I was going to try to find out who this person named 'Tassy' was. My independence would be short lived however because the lies Satan kept whispering in my ear would send me running for the wrong harbor of shelter once again.

"He reached down from on high and took hold of me; he drew me out of deep waters. He rescued me from my powerful enemy, from my foes, who were too strong for me."
Psalm 18:16-17

Chapter 5

Prince Number 3

"She said, I will go after my lovers, who give me my food and my water, my wool and my linen, my oil and my drink"
Hosea 2:5

Eventually I started dating again but because of the deep rejection that was now added to my already low self-esteem you can imagine how vulnerable I was. I was an accident waiting to happen once again! I needed to find that 'prince' from the fairy tale in my head but instead I just kept kissing frogs that always turned into **toads not princes**! My lily pond was **brimful of toads** by this time!

I was in my early forties now and I longed for intimacy with someone who would think I was worth loving. I thought intimacy only meant sex so that was where I would seek the intimacy I needed even though I knew in my spirit according to God's Word it was wrong. I knew what the Bible said about sexual intimacy out of marriage but I just needed someone to validate that I was desirable and that was what I had mistakenly come to believe made you desirable. Ephesians 5:3 says, *"But among you there must not be even a hint of sexual immorality, or of any kind of impurity, or of greed, because these are improper for God's holy people."* I thought sex was the way you got close to someone and made them love you. I needed to fill up that deep hole of loneliness inside that was growing ever bigger. After my last divorce I just felt like an old rag tossed away in the trash heap, an undesirable woman that no one could love.

I vacillated between trying to live God's way and my way but my way was winning out once again. I wanted to live by my flesh because it was screaming out loudly for attention and so I listened to that voice rather than the voice of my Savior. I just needed to quiet the voices in me that were screaming, *"no one wants you, and you are not worth loving"*. I did not understand that most of those voices I was hearing were coming from Satan. Satan has played a huge role in deepening the bondage I have lived in since my childhood. He used the lack of love in childhood to continue to drive the message into my heart that *"I was not worth loving"*. With each failed relationship, Satan deepened my shame, insecurity and self-doubt with haunting accusations of worthlessness. Even though his words were lies, because others had rejected me by their actions I believed his lies were truth that "I was not worth loving". Jesus said in John 8:44 that *"He is a liar and the father of lies"*.

I was willing to use whatever it took, to quiet the voices inside whether it was relationships with men, alcohol, pills, partying or shopping. **OH**—how I especially loved shopping for clothes or things to decorate the house. It gave me that instant happy feeling inside but its effect was very short lived! I thought the clothes would make me look good on the outside to everyone else and then maybe *someone would take notice of me and want me!* The bondage was growing with each failure and crippling me even more but I did not understand it back then. I knew I loved the LORD but I did not know how to live without the pain inside! I did not know how to let God heal my pain. I did not know how to live by the Spirit because I had never been taught how to live that way, not until the last few years. I decided to live in the demands of my flesh because it made me feel better and seemed to quiet the terrible pain that was inside of me, **for a little while anyway**. Galatians 5:16-17 says, *"So I say, live by the Spirit, and you will not gratify the desires of the sinful nature. For the sinful nature desires what is contrary to the Spirit, and the Spirit what is contrary to the sinful nature. They are in conflict with each other, so that you do not do what you want."*

Once again as you can imagine, I experienced many unsuccessful relationships and I just could not find the 'prince' that wanted to rescue me. I was too desperate and needy and I was running most of the descent guys I dated away. That is usually what happens with insecure people; most secure people are able to spot needy desperation a mile away. I did however date one man about a year after my divorce that recognized the insecurity in me and he tried to encourage and show me that I was beautiful and desirable. He made me feel special for the first time in my life and it felt **wonderful**! I fell head over heels in love with him but I was so needy I was a maniac! I was like a long dried out sponge soaking up every bit of moisture I could get and that kind of neediness can quickly suck another person dry. He was recovering from a similar divorce situation, he was not ready to recommit to marriage, and *I was in a hurry to get married*! He had a rescuer personality and I needed rescuing but he just was not ready to rescue me permanently through marriage. I do not blame him for running from me. *I was running from me too!*

Most of my adult life I have suffered with periods of depression. I began to suffer from more severe bouts of depression after the break up of my second marriage and they seemed to increase in frequency and depth. I also suffered from anxiety and a tremendous fear was always present inside of me. There was a horrible voice of fear in me saying, *"You are not going to make it, you cannot make it on your own, you cannot take care of yourself"*. That voice had been there for a long time, **since childhood**. I tried several different brands of antidepressants for my depression and took them off and on for months. I became so depressed at times that I would just lie on the floor in the dark and cry for hours at the time. Many days I did not even want to see the sunshine outside. I liked it better when it was dark and gloomy, *just the way I felt on the inside!*

Satan was in hot pursuit of me whispering his lies to me that I was not loveable and no one wanted me. I just did not understand back then that it was Satan whispering and not my own voice. I did not understand how cunning and subtle Satan is and how he wanted to destroy me at all costs! He was willing to use any means to keep me in bondage and prevent my restoration. Satan is afraid of who we are and what we can become and the power we have over his dark kingdom. *He will stop at nothing to prevent our realizing our power and the destiny God has planned for us.* John 10:10 tells us that Satan comes to kill, steal and destroy us and he was doing a very good job stealing and destroying my life. Satan made sure he kept sending **false comforters** to me in order to deepen my bondage. He knew my weakness was my **great need to feel loved and valuable** and he continued to attack me relentlessly in this vulnerable area. The sad part is I had unknowingly become a willing participant in my own destruction.

When 'prince number three' galloped into the scene in 1995, two years after my divorce, I was ripe for the picking because my heart had not healed yet. I had also just recently broken up with the man I had fallen in love with. 'Prince number three' was very attentive and I was starved for attention. He sent me flowers constantly and two or three cards in the mail every day. He called me long distance everyday, sometimes more than once. He called me sweet names in the beginning, *until after we were married*. He lived about four hours from where I lived and so we only saw each other on the weekends. He **seemed** to be the white knight that would make everything wonderful and we could live 'happily ever after'. However, he was also very insecure and had many emotional issues he was dealing with himself. One of his issues was that he was a recovering alcoholic and had a very strong controlling personality. He was just what I needed once again—someone to take control and take care of me.

I went to Church off and on (more off than on) after my second divorce. I was trying to the best of **my ability** at the time to renew my relationship with the LORD. That was part of the main problem; *I was trying to make the changes and not letting God make them.* I knew the LORD was always with me but I had a **really bad habit** of wandering off on my own, a habit He would begin breaking **for good** in 2004. I needed to find a new church home after the divorce because many of my ex-husband's family went to the church where I had been a member while we were married. Not being grounded in a Church home with loving supportive people around me only added to my isolation and vulnerability to Satan's attacks. *"Let us not give up meeting together, as some are in the habit of doing, but let us encourage one another—and all the more as you see the Day approaching."* (Hebrews 10:25)

When 'prince number three' came to visit he was always eager to go to Church with me and I thought that was a good sign. I knew I needed to marry someone that was a Christian and he *seemed* to fit that mold. He was another 'take charge' kind of guy which was what I wanted at the time. I needed someone to take care of me because I did not think I was doing a very good job. I was struggling financially even though all of bills were being paid. I was not making a lot of extra money and so I was not able to pay off the rest of my debts. The LORD was faithfully providing for my needs but not enough of "my wants" so I was looking for a man who could do that for me. I just did not trust the LORD enough to let Him be all I needed at the time.

My emptiness was still there and it needed to be satisfied by whatever means I could find and buying things always seemed to make me feel better. This new prince was always buying me things and that was part of the bait that Satan used to lure me into another unhealthy relationship. Due to this 'prince's' insecurity he thought that the only way to win a woman was by giving her things. I guess he did not think he had anything else he could offer her. He treated me just like my mother and the last husband I had, giving things in the place of real love.

I realize I was trusting in this man's riches instead of in my Heavenly Father's provisions. Haggai 2:8 says, "*'The silver is mine and the gold is mine,' declares the LORD Almighty.*" I did not have enough faith to trust that the LORD could provide whatever I needed materially. God was trying to teach me that lesson but I did not want to learn it back then. I wanted results immediately and this man could provide them so I chose what I thought was the easy way. I wanted financial security and to be a stay at home wife so I could paint and he could provide me with that kind of life.

Three months after we started dating he proposed to me and tried to give me a huge diamond engagement ring. I was not sure I wanted to accept his marriage proposal. Something in my spirit was telling me no, this was not the man God wanted me to marry and I was not sure it was the man I wanted to marry either. I had been praying a lot about the relationship and it seemed the more I prayed, "LORD remove him if he was not the right one for me" the harder he ran after me. It is clear to me now that it was Satan and not the LORD causing the "hot pursuit". I told him no because we hadn't known each other long enough even though I desperately wanted to be married again. I finally gave in to his proposal however two months later even though I did not have peace inside about my decision. I was still having anxiety attacks and suffering from depression and they even seemed to be worse when I was around him. I was too blinded by my fear of being alone to acknowledge the reason I felt worse around him—*I should not have married him*! I had not really gotten over the man I was in love with and had recently broken up with. He was still constantly in the back of my mind because he was the first man that had been nice to me in a long time! I was too **self-centered** to see that I was not just affecting my life by marrying this 'prince number three' but his as well.

After about a month of being engaged, I broke up with him and gave back the ring. We had gone on a trip to meet some of his family and I witnessed his unprovoked violent temper a couple of times. This sent up some red flags on the inside of me and I decided I should not marry him. I had been praying very hard and seeking an answer from the LORD about marrying this man and had asked the LORD to show me a clear sign of His will. The night we returned from our trip, I just knew deep inside I was not supposed to marry him and so I called off the engagement. I left that next morning to return home to Florence. I knew I did not love him the way I should and I really wanted to follow the LORD'S will for me.

During the time we were dating, I had been reading a book by a well-known Christian writer that contained in it a story about an answer to prayer. The person had asked God to give him two visual signs of confirmation to an answer he was seeking so I decided to pray for the same thing in my decision about this marriage. I prayed this prayer before we left on our trip, "God would you please give me two visual signs about my decision to marry this man". I looked the whole time we were on the trip but I did not see anything like I was expecting. I was looking for a visual sign like falling stars or something which is what this writer experienced. I realized much later that I did see the two signs I had asked for while we were on the trip; they were the two terrible unprovoked outbursts of anger from this man. I received my two visual signs as confirmation about my decision **after** I broke the engagement and was on my way home. Isaiah 7:11 says, *"Ask the LORD your God for a sign, whether in the deepest depths or in the highest heights."* The LORD does not always give us visual signs the way he did in the Old Testament days because we now have His Word to guide us. However, God's Word says in Hebrews 13:8, *"Jesus Christ is the same yesterday and today and forever."* Since the man in the book I was reading had received his answer visually I decided I would ask the Father to do the same for me. *I am a visual kind of girl!* I can tell you for a fact that He does still perform signs and wonders today, just as He did for the Saints of the Old Testament, because He has so many times in my life.

It was early in the morning when I left for home and there was a beautiful clear blue sky overhead and not a cloud anywhere in the sky. Before I left I prayed for a safe trip home and asked the LORD to tell me if I had made the right decision. I had driven about ten miles out of town when I looked out of my left side window and there in the sky was a **huge** *pillar shaped cloud* that looked almost like a slender white tornado in the sky. I had never seen any cloud like it before in my life. It was there all by itself in the sky with no other clouds around. Immediately I thought of the *pillar of cloud* that the LORD guided the Israelites with during their wilderness journey out of Egypt. I had been reading and studying a lot about the Israelites and their journey and so it was very fresh in my mind. It says in Exodus 13:21-22, *"By day the LORD went ahead of them in a pillar of cloud to guide them on their way and by night in the pillar of fire to give them light, so that they could travel by day or night. Neither the pillar of cloud by day nor the pillar of fire by night left its place in front of the people."* I must admit I was a little freaked out when I first saw this *pillar of cloud*! I think the first thing that I said was, *"Is that you LORD?"* Then as I drove along an even more amazing thing happened, the cloud was staying right beside me, it did not move, change shape or dissipate. It was almost as if it was *following me*! I know this probably sounds **crazy** to you because I promise you it seemed **crazy** to me at the time! The *pillar of cloud* stayed there for about five miles and then it was gone. As amazing as the appearance was I remember saying to the LORD, **"Okay this could be from you, but LORD I asked for two signs and that was only one cloud."**

    I continued to ponder this phenomenon as I drove wondering what it meant. About two hours later I looked out of my side window again and there in the clear blue sky was another *pillar cloud* **exactly** like the first one! Well I almost ran over the median this time when I saw it! This second cloud was just as big as the first one and continued to follow me and remain unchanged for about the same distance. I was **sure this time** that it had been put there in the sky by God as a sign to me that I had made the right decision.

When I arrived home I **immediately** went inside and looked in my Bible in Exodus to read once again about the *pillar of cloud* that God gave the Israelites during their journey to the Promised Land. The purpose of the *pillars of cloud and fire* was to protect the Israelites from their enemies, control their movements, and provide reassurance of God's presence with them. God used the *two pillars of cloud* in my life for the exact same reasons. He was reassuring me that I was going in the right direction and He was with me. I had asked for two signs and the LORD gave me the *two pillars of cloud*.

Well, you guessed it; I did not stay on the LORD'S path for long! This 'prince' continued to pursue me. He kept calling me and said he was concerned about me and checking to make sure, I was okay. A few weeks later, I came down with a bad case of the flu and because I did not have any family in town, I was feeling pretty lonely and blue. My mother had died in 1988, my daughter was away at college at the time and I had no other family living close by. He called one day and said he wanted to come down and take me to the beach to try to help me feel better. He knew how I loved the ocean and said it might cheer me up. While we were there, he was so caring and concerned and I was so vulnerable. He proposed again and I accepted. He just happened to have the ring sent to the condo where we were staying and I fell—**hook, line and sinker**! *"But they soon forgot what he had done and did not wait for his counsel."* (Psalm 106:13) I made my own plans once more and did not heed what the Spirit of the LORD was trying to tell me. This little sheep wandered off on her own path once again! *"We all, like sheep have gone astray, each of us has turned to his own way."* Isaiah 53:6

We planned the perfect **'fairy tale wedding'** in the Bahamas and I was so sure that at last I had found 'Prince Charming'—complete with a new coach. He wanted to buy me a brand new BMW Z3 sports car for my wedding present and I thought I was truly living in a **'fairy tale'**. I finally got my beautiful formal wedding that every little girl dreams about; complete with the long beaded white gown, bridesmaids and flowers set in a tropical paradise. He even rented a white Rolls Royce for my wedding coach. I finally felt like the **'fairy princess'** in the fairy tales I had loved as a child. I was even able to admit that I looked beautiful because *I felt beautiful* in my long white wedding gown. I had never received so much attention and it was wonderful! I was living in a dream that would soon turn into a nightmare—immediately after the wedding reception for crying aloud!

In the white Rolls Royce limousine on the way back to the hotel, I realized I had married the wrong man again! For really no reason at all he yelled at me in a hostile tone and said, "I'm sick of your "G d #**#". I will never forget the look in the limo driver's eyes in the rear view mirror. His eyes were as big as saucers and they seemed to say to me, *"Girl are you sure you know what you are doing?"* I knew somewhere down in my spirit I should have told the driver, "Please take me to the courthouse so that I can have this marriage annulled immediately, it was a mistake"! I just did not have the courage to do it. I was too proud to admit I had made another mistake and too ashamed to admit failure once again, **so I kept quiet.**

This marriage was doomed for failure from the beginning. I married him for the wrong reason, to take care of me and not because I was really in love with him and he was who God wanted me to marry. His anger toward me right after the wedding caused me to distance myself from him immediately.

I could not believe I had done it again! I had married another "Dr. Jekyll and Mr. Hyde" but I was going to stick it out and try and make it work. It seemed that nothing I ever did was right and I never knew what kind of mood he was going to be in. Some days he just got up mad and I didn't know why and when I asked him about it he just seemed to get madder.

I had moved away from all of my friends when we got married and I did not know a single person in the town where he lived so I felt terribly isolated and alone. My depression started to come back after our marriage and my subsequent move from Florence. I could not seem to shake it on my own so I went to a doctor and he started me back on antidepressants to help pull me out of the depression.

Many things happened during the first few months of our marriage that continued to deepen my depression. About five months after we were married I became physically afraid of him after one such incident. He became violently angry with me because of a remark I made to him and he shoved a chair out from under me. Trust me; it was not a remark worthy of that kind of abuse! All the terrible names he called me were very demeaning and so I once again withdrew into a world of isolation and depression.

In February of 1997 my depression had worsened to unbelievable depths of hopelessness. I felt trapped and I was so miserable! I decided to go to a lawyer and see what my options were if I got a divorce. The day before we got married I had signed a pre-nuptial agreement which I did not want to do. He had discussed such an agreement before the marriage and I told him that, "if he really knew me and trusted me he would not need me to sign such an agreement". That should have been another warning sign to me that this was not the right marriage for me! Without going into any details there was not going to be much help for me financially because we had only been married for six months. I now had an expensive car that had over $400.00 a month payments and I did not know how I would pay for it. When we met I owned a nice mustang convertible that was paid for and when he bought me this new car I sold it at his request. I had lived without a car before for three years and I just could not do that again. The financial information I received from the lawyer concerning a divorce only added to my hopelessness and pushed me over the edge.

In my pain and hopelessness, I decided that the only way out was to take an overdose of sleeping tablets. I was so depressed and no one seemed to notice my pain. I kept wondering how could I be living in such darkness and no one understand the pain I was in. The only way I can describe how I was feeling is that I felt like I was in a **deep dark hole** that was sucking me under and I could not seem to climb out. I hurt so bad emotionally I could not breathe! *I just wanted the darkness to stop no matter what I had to do to stop it!*

I went to the store a few hours after I left the attorney's office and bought two boxes of over the counter sleeping tablets. I realized that because I was depressed the doctor would probably not write me a prescription for sleeping pills. I went home and fixed myself a strong vodka drink and then proceeded to drink several more because I needed the courage to do what I was about to do. Alcohol always helps to loosen your inhibitions and I was counting on that to give me my courage to take the pills.

After he came home from work, we got into a heated discussion about a divorce and it was going nowhere fast! He was being mean and cold to me so I proceeded to take the pills that I had in the pocket of my pajamas in his presence. It must have been around 8:30 p.m. when I took the pills. He just laughed and said, "Go ahead that's a real smart thing for you to do" and then watched me swallow them. In fairness to him I must tell you he did call a friend of his who was a dentist and asked him what was going to happen to me after I took the pills and he told him that it would just give me a bad hangover effect. That however turned out not to be a very accurate diagnosis! When I started feeling woozy, I went upstairs, looked for some more pills to take but I did not find any. I then went and lay down on the bed. He said that a few minutes later, *"something"* made him go upstairs and check on me and when he turned on the light I was unconscious and my eyes had rolled back in my head. That *"something"* that made him go upstairs to check on me I believe was God, He was not going to allow Satan to take my life. Isaiah 54:17 (KJV) says, *"No weapon that is formed against you will prosper."*

My husband called 911 for an ambulance to take me to the hospital and at that point my pulse was very weak. The next thing I remember was being in the emergency room and the doctor was talking to me and trying to make me wake up and talk. I tried to answer the doctor's questions but I could not form my words, I kept falling back to sleep. I kept wondering what was going on, *where was I?* I was told they had pumped out my stomach twice. I started vomiting the charcoal they had given me to absorb the drugs and I had black stuff all over my hands and face. I was having a difficult time staying awake, my head was so heavy and everything was foggy. I just wanted them to leave me alone! Then they moved me into another room where there were two nurses who **treated me very mean**. I wondered why they were being so mean to me. Then I started to remember that I had taken the pills. I figured out later that they were mean to me because it was their job to save lives and I had just tried to end mine.

I don't **ever** remember feeling as sick as I did that night. My throat and esophagus felt like they were on fire. You see, when they pump your stomach they run a tube through your nose down into your stomach and feed the charcoal mixture into the tube and suck the contents out of your stomach. My reason for being so graphic about what they did to me is in the hope that it will prevent others from going through this same ***horrible nightmare***! I am so thankful that I was not conscious when they performed that lovely procedure! The toxins from the pills I took had absorbed into my body by now and had made every bone in my body ache.

In my hazy memory of that night when I woke up again, it was Wednesday morning, I was in a room with two single beds, and there were mesh bars over the windows. I was so disoriented I did not know where I was or how I got there and *I just wanted to go home.* It didn't look like a hospital room. A doctor came in to run an EKG on me, and I told him I wanted to go home. He said I was not going home for at least two weeks because I had tried to commit suicide. I was on the psychiatric floor and I would have to have some counseling before I could go home. **I was scared to death!** I was living in a strange city where I had no close friends with a strange man that obviously did not care about me and now I was locked away in a strange hospital on the psych ward. ***Oh my God, what was going to happen to me!*** I began thinking they were never going to let me go home or that my husband would leave me up there locked away forever. All kinds of terrible thoughts went through my mind. On a scale of one to ten of frightening experiences, I would have to say it rated a **twelve!**

My husband was supposed to go out of town that day but he postponed his trip. He asked me what items I needed him to bring to me in the hospital and the first thing I told him I needed was my **Bible**. I knew the LORD was still with me and only He could help me now in this terrible hour. *"The LORD is with me; I will not be afraid. What can man do to me?"* (Psalm 118:6) I cried out to Him in prayer for help and told Him how frightened I was and that I needed His help. He answered me amazingly with a direct word from Psalm 116. As soon as I received my Bible I just opened it randomly to read but when I looked down and began to read the pages where I had opened, *I knew the LORD had directed the pages*. It was no coincidence that I had opened my Bible to Psalm 116—it was a "God-incidence". It described exactly the nightmare that I just experienced and I knew the LORD was speaking tenderly to me through this Psalm. I would like to share with you the words the LORD shared with me that day in my dark hour of need.

"I love the LORD, for he heard my voice; he heard my cry for mercy. Because he turned his ear to me, I will call on him as long as I live. The cords of death entangled me, the anguish of the grave came upon me; I was overcome by trouble and sorrow. Then I called on the name of the LORD; 'O LORD, save me!' The LORD is gracious and righteous; our God is full of compassion. The LORD protects the simple hearted; when I was in great need, he saved me. Be at rest once more, O my soul, for the LORD has been good to you. For you, O LORD, have delivered my soul from death, my eyes from tears, my feet from stumbling, that I may walk before the LORD in the land of the living. I believed; therefore I said, 'I am greatly afflicted.' And in my dismay I said, 'All men are liars.' How can I repay the LORD for all his goodness to me? I will lift up the cup of salvation and call on the name of the LORD. I will fulfill my vows to the LORD in the presence of all his people. Precious in the sight of the LORD is the death of his saints. O LORD, truly

I am your servant, the son of your maidservant; you have freed me from my chains." Psalm 116:1-16

After I read this Psalm I started to weep uncontrollably with such a sweet release and then an ***incredible peace came over me***. There are not adequate words to describe to you the **powerful presence** of the LORD with me in my hospital room that day. I felt His comforting arms wrap around me calming the fear in my heart. I asked the LORD what was I supposed to do now, how could I bear staying in this horrible place for two weeks? I heard so clearly the LORD'S voice in a still small whisper say to me, "Just do what they tell you to do, get up and get dressed, go to your sessions and you will not have to stay here that long". I decided to obey the LORD and trust Him with the rest. *"He will have no fear of bad news; his heart is steadfast, trusting in the LORD." (Psalm 112:7)*

There was a young girl in the room with me and she was suffering from a deep depression as well. I began to try and talk with her and she shared with me that this was not her first visit here and she had small children at home that needed her. She would just lay there and not get dressed or go to her sessions so I started encouraging her to get up, get dressed and cooperate so she could get well and go home to her children who needed her. She finally listened to me and started doing better. I believe that my reaching out and ministering to her helped to speed up the process for my release. The LORD was faithful to His promise of my not staying there for very long. The doctor released me to go home on Saturday morning, just three days later. **Amazing!** No, it was **a miracle**! It was almost unheard of for someone who had attempted suicide to be released that soon.

My doctor changed my antidepressant medication and I agreed to attend counseling sessions as part of my early release.

The doctor told me because of the history of my mother's depression and my chemical imbalance that it was possible that I might have to remain on antidepressants the rest of my life. I trusted that he knew what he was talking about. However, I developed a stronghold of fear that I could never live normally without taking antidepressants. I questioned him about the fact that I was taking them when I attempted my suicide. His explanation for that was that they were not the right kind of antidepressants for me and I needed one that supplied both brain chemicals that my brain was not producing. A new brand that had just been released on the market would provide both the chemicals I needed so I should not have any more problems, according to my doctor. The new prescription worked great in the beginning. I was lifted out of the darkness that engulfed me and I felt like smiling for the first time in so long. It had been a long time since I had felt so good; I did not feel like I was riding an emotional roller coaster any longer.

A week after my release from the hospital I started my counseling sessions with a wonderful Christian woman counselor. I learned a lot from my counseling sessions, mainly that I needed to learn how to stand up for myself and I did not need to let other people control my life. I learned from her *I did not deserve the bad treatment that I was allowing in my life.*

Right after my suicide attempt, my husband and I seemed to get along a little better but then when I started refusing his abusive treatment and not letting him control me anymore, he was not very happy. Our marriage just got steadily worse and more distant with time. We were just two roommates sharing the same house just like my last marriage. I was sleeping in one bedroom and he was sleeping in another. We had not had any sexual contact with each other for a long time. In the back of my mind was the memory of him just standing there letting me swallow the sleeping pills and I did not want to be intimate with someone who did not care if I lived or died. His anger became more frequent and after our second year anniversary, I decided to divorce him and admit my failure. We just could not live together anymore; the hostility was too much for me.

In the beginning, the divorce proceedings were ugly but eventually we became friendlier. The first time I moved out of the house, believe it or not, my second husband actually came and helped me move. I think he felt he owed it to me after all of the **hell** he had put me through during our divorce. *What a nightmare the move was!* I had two twenty-four foot long moving trucks 'packed to the max' and just a few miles outside of town we had trouble with both of them. Then after driving for almost six hours to my destination, we finally arrived at the house and had to unload the trucks in a **horrendous thunderstorm.** Needless to say that was the last time he volunteered to help me move!

After about four months of separation I started to panic, I did not think I could make it on my own. I missed the security of someone taking care of me, the trips to the Bahamas we used to take, the ballgames we used to go. I missed the 'father figure' he was in my life. The memories of how miserable our relationship was had started to fade and I did not want to be alone. We talked several times and decided to try to reconcile. I even moved everything back to his town and into his house but within less than a week, we knew the marriage was not going to work. So he helped me moved out the second time. Even though he had many issues in his life that needed healing and changing, I know I was also a very hard person to live with too! I had married him for all of the wrong reasons.

As I look back now I realize Satan was using this man to pull me down once again so he could try to destroy me. If he could keep me paralyzed in bondage then he could render me ineffective in my relationship with the LORD. He could then keep me from doing anything effective for God's Kingdom. Satan was succeeding in all of these endeavors.

Before my second divorce, I had been very active in teaching small children in a mission's class that was growing rapidly. I was also growing in my relationship with the LORD. I was becoming a threat to Satan's Kingdom and so he worked through my husband to try to destroy me. 1 Peter 5:8 (KJV) tells us, *"Be sober, be vigilant, because your adversary, the devil, like a roaring lion walketh about, seeking whom he may devour"*. Unfortunately, I have heard his savage ferocious roar much too often in my life! Satan is so cunning; he knows our every weakness and waits to attack again, when and where we are most vulnerable. *"And no wonder, for Satan himself masquerades as an angel of light."* (2 Corinthians 11:14) After the second divorce I was again growing in my closeness to the LORD, something Satan did not want to see happen.

Once again Satan sought out my vulnerable area, the need for love and a man to take care of me and he was successful in causing my fall. I did not have enough faith and trust to believe that the LORD could take care of me better than any human man was able to do. I did not **stand firm in my faith** and so I came crashing down once again. Isaiah 7:9 says, *"If you do not stand firm in your faith, you will not stand at all."* Oh how important it is to have unwavering faith, believe God's Word is truth and obey His commands.

"'Woe to the obstinate children,' declares the LORD, 'to those who carry out plans that are not mine, forming an

alliance, but not by my Spirit, heaping sin upon sin; who go down to Egypt without consulting me; who look for help to Pharaoh's protection, to Egypt's shade for refuge."
Isaiah 30:1-3

Chapter 6

Prince Number 4

"It is better to take refuge in the Lord than to trust in man. It is better to take refuge in the Lord than to trust in princes."
Psalm 118:8-9

Instead of moving back home to Florence when 'prince number three' and I separated the first time I decided I wanted to live near the beach. I had grown up near the ocean most of my life and I loved the peace the sea brings to my soul. There was also another reason I did not want to move back to Florence, *I was embarrassed and my pride was hurt.* I was having a hard time accepting that I was divorced for the third time and I was not ready to face anyone I knew. **How could this be happening to me?** I just could not believe there was no one that could love me the way I needed to be loved. Why was that such a hard thing to find? Why were there not any good men out there that would just accept and love me? I was blinded to the reality of my brokenness inside and that the reason my relationships kept failing was because **"of me"**—not just the men I picked.

Let me clearly state that my unhealthy choices of men contributed **a lot** to the failed relationships too. Many of my relationship choices also put me in situations that were doomed for failure. My desperation for someone to love me had grown into a stronghold that was all consuming. It seemed that everywhere I went I was constantly looking for 'prince charming'. *I had become obsessed with finding a man, any man to love me*! I just had to find him; I could not stand this ache inside that was growing larger with every failure.

After we separated, I was going to be okay financially for a while if I managed my money wisely (something I had not yet learned how to do). I was going to receive $2,000 in alimony each month for two years (the number of months we were married) according to the terms of the pre-nuptial agreement. We sold my engagement ring to pay off my car so I would not have a car payment.

The first time we separated in July of 1998 I came home and went down to Myrtle Beach with my friend Kitty to look for a place to live. We started looking at North Myrtle Beach but I ended up renting a house on the southern end in the small quaint seaport town of Georgetown, South Carolina.

In December of 1998, after our second separation, I went back to Georgetown, rented a really cute duplex in the historic district and started my life over once again! I felt like Abraham when God told him to go and he did not know where he was going. *"The LORD had said to Abram, 'Leave your country, your people and your father's household and go to the land I will show you."* (Genesis 12:1) I did not know a single person in Georgetown but I knew that was where God had led me and He had opened the door for some reason. His purpose in moving me there was to begin my journey to the deep emotional healing I had needed for so long.

I met new friends and found a wonderful Church home in Georgetown. The Pastor and his wife were so kind and friendly and all of the people in the Church took me in under their wings and loved me so tenderly. To this day I still have a very special place in my heart for that sweet loving Church and the Pastor and his wife have remained very dear friends of mine. I loved my little apartment and life was good for a while until the loneliness and feeling of rejection once again set in **like a thick fog**. I tried to stay busy painting and visiting with friends but that **unquenchable thirst** to be loved by a man was returning. I also went to Florence frequently to deliver paintings and visit with some of my close friends I had missed during the past two years. During one of my trips to Florence in 1999 was when I first saw the "woman at the well" statue in a cemetery that I passed. That is a day I will be forever grateful for because of the part the statue played in my eventual healing of my *broken and shattered heart*.

After living in Georgetown about four months 'prince number four' rode into my life wielding his sword of attention to rescue me from my tower of loneliness. This time Satan was oh so clever, he used a man with the **same last name** as my father for crying aloud! *How is that one for clever?* This 'prince' even had beautiful silver hair just like my father. That memory must have stayed tucked away in my subconscious because I was always drawn to look at beautiful silver haired men. Something clicked inside of me and I just knew he was the one I had been waiting for all of my life, **a man like my father!**

Satan knew he had to be cleverer this time to snare me because I was more aware now, after my counseling, of the type of controlling abusive men I had chosen in the past. He knew I would shy away from anyone that was too controlling so he used a totally opposite type personality. This 'prince' was very passive, a total opposite on the scale of temperaments than most all of the other men I had chosen in the past. He was also a born again Christian and I knew this was what the LORD wanted for me. I failed to ask the LORD however if it was His will that I marry this man, I just assumed it was. This man was in the process of a divorce from a long marriage and was feeling rejected too. There we were two magnets drawn together for more disaster and I fell **(no jumped!)** right into Satan's trap once again.

I married 'prince number four' about five months after we met. I did not wait long to get married this time either, which seemed to be my pattern. Maybe because of my inferiority I thought if they waited too long they would change their mind about me. Once again, I looked to someone else to take care of me and fill my loneliness instead of the LORD.

We got married in the small chapel of my Church there in Georgetown. We had a small ceremony and his three small children were in the wedding. We also rented a big house so we would have more room for his children to come and stay on the weekends. I continued to paint full time but we were struggling financially. My alimony stopped when we got married and I lost a whole year of support, $24,000.00 to be exact! He was also self-employed in sales but was not making a lot of money either. The stupidity of what I had done did not matter though because I finally had the family I had always wanted and I just knew this was going to finally be **"my happily ever after"**.

Well, it did not take long for the honeymoon to be over, *exactly two days after we were married*. His ex-wife telephoned and made plans for us to keep the children for ten days while she went on a trip out of the country. He did not even discuss it with me before he agreed to keep them and *I was not a happy camper*. His decision did not sit well with me because he didn't even talk to me about it before he told her yes. I wanted to be the center of his world and I had never even considered that his children would come before me.

During our few months of marriage he never discussed anything about the children with me, especially when they were coming to stay with us. I thought that was an **important detail**—I should have been included in these plans! This pattern continued for the rest of our marriage, which by the way only lasted from September until the next April. He told me in so many words that his children would always come first in his life and once again, *I felt a terrible sense of rejection*. We even tried counseling but nothing changed and so we decided to separate and end the marriage. I knew I had rushed into this marriage **too quickly** and that I had made a terrible mistake. I thought that I obviously was not worth fighting for because he had given up so easily and so I moved out of the house in May and into an apartment just seven months after we were married.

A few months after we were married, God revealed to me the real reason He had brought me to Georgetown. I was under the mistaken impression that the reason God had led me there was to find this 'prince'. Instead, God had led me there so that He could heal me, through a prayer-counseling ministry, from the terrible hurt I had suffered as a child due to my father's sudden death. Through a series of God inspired circumstances (God-instances as I call them), I met a girl who introduced me to a married couple who worked for a Christian ministry that traveled all over the world helping to heal people of the hurts left from childhood. This girl who I became friends with had been working with this couple to heal the wounds left in her own life from childhood. As she and I talked, I shared my past with her and we decided that I should make an appointment to see them. I knew there was a lot of hurt inside of me and I was willing to **do anything** to find help and healing. Even during the times that I was married, I still lived with a haunting fear inside that said *"I was not safe and I was not going to make it"*.

A couple of days before my appointment the counselors gave me a set of tapes to listen to and a questionnaire to complete before our session. I must admit I was a little skeptical about the whole thing at first but as I sat and listened to the tapes I knew somewhere in my spirit that this was something that was going to **"set me free"**. This was a divine appointment that had been arranged for me by my Heavenly Father minutes after my father's death. *"All the days ordained for me were written in your book before one of them came to be."* (Psalm 139:16) In the fullness of time God had led me here for my long overdue healing. While I was preparing for the healing session, the man and wife couple were also preparing by fasting and praying for God to reveal to them the cause of my brokenness.

The morning of my appointment arrived and I was **very nervous**. I did not know what to expect but I knew that I was not going to miss this appointment for *anything in the world*. During the first half of the day I shared with my counselors my life story. They questioned me extensively about my childhood and all of the relationships in my life. Much of what I shared was very painful, things I had not wanted to share with anyone before. I felt like I was sitting in a Catholic confessional sharing all of my deep dark sins with a Priest. They told me before we started that unless I was open and honest with them about everything the healing would not be effective.

I had learned from the tapes I listened to before my session that when people are wounded as children and the hurt is not healed that it remains stuffed deep down inside. Unless the wound is dealt with and healed, it will continue to grow and then begin to manifest itself on the outside in a variety of ways.

It can show up in a number of ways such as various forms of addiction, anger, low self-esteem, fear, obsessive-compulsive behavior, depression, perfectionism and eventually physical forms of sickness. I realized I was experiencing *many of these manifestations* and I wanted healing. I did not understand at the time however that all of these would not be healed instantly. God was going to have to peel them off like an onion, one layer at the time.

We took a lunch break, during which time the couple discussed what they had learned. They prayed for knowledge on how to proceed with my healing. They had discerned from the Holy Spirit that my pain was coming from the loss of my father and that I had never experienced the closure of his death. When we came back together, they placed two chairs side by side facing in opposite directions. The man sat in one chair and I sat in the other. He told me he was going to sit in the place of my father and that he was going to put his arms around me and hold me like my father. He wanted me to pretend he was my father and say whatever was on my heart that I needed to say to my father. As soon as he put his arms around me and started to talk softly to me, I *burst into huge crocodile tears*! I cried and cried for what seemed like hours! *I cried a puddle of tears onto the floor*! Psalm 56:8 tells us that God puts our tears in a bottle and I am here to tell you He needed a tractor trailer to hold all of the bottles I filled that day! I will never forget the feeling of **sweet release** I experienced. The best way that I can describe to you how it felt was that my heart was like the cork on a champagne bottle that someone just popped opened. The release of pressure inside was **incredible** and it continued to flow out in the form of loud sobs and huge tears for about an hour. I do not remember anything I said but I do remember hearing him say, "Baby, I'm sorry I couldn't come home to you, it wasn't because I didn't love you but because I got in a bad accident. I loved you very much and I'm sorry it has caused you so much pain. Please forgive me. I love you." *The healing that took place that day was nothing short of miraculous!*

When I was finally able to turn off the floodgate of tears and gain my composure, we repeated the same procedure only this time the woman was taking the place of my mother. The difference was **amazing** because there were no emotions or tears this time. The anger I was still carrying inside *only involved the death of my father*. Even though the treatment I received from mother was abusive and painful, I had already dealt with my forgiveness of her years ago before she died in the nursing home.

I learned from my experience that day that the little girl in me had never grown up after her daddy's untimely death. *She was still waiting for her daddy to come home, to love and take care of her again.* I never had the proper kind of closure after his death and so it left a terrible fear and insecurity inside me, it left me always waiting for his return. *A return that was never possible! My daddy was gone from me forever and now forty-three years later I was finally able to bury him.*

The outpouring of pent up emotions left me drained and exhausted. The counselors told me that I would probably sleep a lot for the next few days due to the depth of the emotional experience. They also told me that it was natural for me to continue to cry off and on for a month or so because my heart was still in the process of healing. Just like a wound continues to ooze after an injury, my mending heart oozed with healing tears in the days that followed. My body felt like I had run a twenty mile marathon and so I went to bed immediately when I returned home late that afternoon and I slept soundly well into the next day. *Words cannot describe to you the way I felt inside.*

The **'haunting fear'** that had plagued me inside since childhood **was gone!** *The ghost of my father's death had vanished and the pain of his death had been healed but the baggage of my damaged emotions remained.* I was left with the feeling for the first time in my life that *"I was going to be okay, I could make it on my own"*. There was still **plenty** of emotional healing yet to be done by the Lord. The mountain of insecurity in me was still present and growing ever larger.

I am now able to accept part of the blame for the failure of this fourth marriage which is something I could not do at the time. My brokenness had developed in me a ravenous need for attention that was humanly impossible for **anyone** to fulfill. I can see clearly now, that I was jealous of the attention he gave his children because I was so needy and I wanted all of his attention and more. I was so miserable inside and so I made him miserable too! I did not want to be jealous of his children but I could not help myself and I did not understand why, *not until recently when God started healing my wounds*. I did not have enough room left in my heart to care about his children because it was too full of pain. I so desperately needed to be loved by someone that I could not think of anyone but myself and the love I needed. I did not know how to love myself either! I did not know how to receive God's love, even though I had received His forgiveness through salvation. I did not have enough love in me to give away to others.

At the time of this fourth marriage, I had gotten to the point that I needed **constant** strokes of attention and compliments in order to make me feel good about myself. As much as I craved positive affirmation from others, when people did compliment me, I could not just say "thank you" because it embarrassed me. *I did not think I deserved the nice things people said about me.* I could only respond to their compliments with derogatory comments about myself because of what I believed about my own self worth. Even when I looked at myself in the mirror, all I could see was ugliness and imperfection. I was so filled with shame at who I had become I could not look anyone in the eye when I talked with them for fear they would see the **real me** behind the veil I was wearing. *I was such a tangled up mess!* Oh Praise God, he knew the cries of my heart and my deliverance from darkness was certain to come at the **appointed time**.

I continued to seek the LORD'S help and read the Bible after we separated because it was the only thing that brought comfort to my bleeding heart. *"As a mother comforts her child, so will I comfort you."* (Isaiah 66:13) I continued to attend my Church there in Georgetown but slowly I started withdrawing into my shell of self-pity and isolation. I knew that God had orchestrated my appointment for healing from my father's death and so I was looking to Him to help me with the rest of the pain inside. I wanted the pain to go away but I just did not know how to find the deep healing that was needed. I thought that it was something I had to do on my own by making better choices and self-talk. I did not understand that my healing could only take place if I yielded totally to the LORD **my helplessness** in doing anything at all! **Only the LORD** could mend the huge holes in my heart and teach me how to overcome the pain. These are lessons the LORD would start teaching me in 2004 when my house of cards came crashing down.

In 1998 I had purchased a small Women's Devotional Bible that I read from most of the time. I read a lot in the Psalms during these days after the separation because they were so comforting and full of hope and peace. On June 8, 2000, I wrote in this Bible on the first page of the Psalms the following statement: *"Dear God, My prayer is to become a woman after your own heart like King David was!"* I can tell you most assuredly that now four years later God has answered my request by putting a fire in my heart for Him and I am chasing after Him to know Him with all of my might.

During my last months in Georgetown, I continued to paint portraits and tried to stay busy so that I could drown out the voices that were screaming inside of me. My life there seemed over and as I continued to seek the LORD in prayer I felt Him telling me my time in Georgetown was over, it was time to move back to Florence, and so I obeyed.

"In the time of my favor I will answer you, and in the day of salvation I will help you; I will keep you and make you to be a covenant for the people to restore the land and to reassign its desolate inheritances, to say to the captives, 'Come out' and to those in darkness, 'Be free!'".
(Isaiah 49:8-9)

Chapter 7

Running from the Father

"Not long after that, the younger son got together all he had, set off for a distant country and there squandered his wealth in wild living."
Luke 15:13

Five months after my separation from 'prince number four', I packed up my belongings and moved back home to Florence in October of 2000. I rented a townhouse apartment in the same complex building where I lived before I moved away four years earlier. I was still painting portraits full time and most of my work came from Florence during the time I lived in Georgetown. I convinced myself at the time that the reason I was moving back to Florence was for my art business since I never received any commissions from Georgetown anyway. I realize now it was not the reason I moved. I loved Georgetown and had come to love many of the friends I made there but *I was really running from another failure again.* It was a small town and I did not want to have to run into my ex-husband all the time. I was just like the 'woman at the well' who went to draw her water during the heat of the day because she knew no one else would be around at that time of day with their judging glances of disapproval. *She just could not handle any more rejection and neither could I!*

In less than six years, I had been married and divorced three times, moved seven times and now I was starting over one more time! *That has to be some kind of record!* That in itself is enough to cause anyone to suffer emotional damage—probably a little brain damage too! When you add the rest of the baggage that I was already carrying you have enough weight to sink a battleship. I was not finished loading that battleship of brokenness with baggage just yet either!

My heart was wounded to the core. I had married a Christian man this time and it turned out even worse than the others did. Our marriage did not even last a year! I was so angry with everyone—him, God and myself! I was a walking zombie, numb inside but yet full of pain. I felt undesirable and unloved and thought who would want me now that I was divorced for the fourth time! *Oh that sounded horrible!* I decided that I would just not tell anyone about the fourth marriage because three did not sound as bad as four did and besides very few people in Florence knew about this last marriage anyway. How could I have made such a bad choice again! *Who was this crazy woman living in me that had messed up my life so badly anyway?* I decided I must just be a "jerk magnet"! I must have it written on my forehead or something, *"all you bad guys come and get me"*! I do not know how in the world I was even able to function. In reality, I guess I did not function very well, **especially** not as a child of the **Most High God**!

Over the next couple of months I settled into my new life, single again and feeling terribly alone and rejected. I continued painting full time at home for about a year, which only increased my isolation. I renewed many of my old friendships and eventually made some new ones too. At first I did not find a Church to attend in Florence because I was mad at God, and that was the first mistake that would lead me in the wrong direction. I loved my Church in Georgetown and that was the excuse I gave myself for not going to any of the Churches in Florence.

I never completely stopped reading my Bible or praying but my heart was not really in it because I blamed God for my bad life. I want you to understand clearly that I never stopped loving the LORD or being grateful for my salvation but *I* wanted to be in control of my own life and not **Him**. I talked a lot about how much I loved the LORD and the things He had done for me in my life but I was just *"talking the talk and not walking the walk"*! I was a hypocrite of the worst kind—my heart was far from Him because of my inner anger. *"But then they would flatter him with their mouths, lying to him with their tongues; their hearts were not loyal to him, they were not faithful to his covenant."* (Psalm 78:37)

Deep inside I felt that if I was His child how could He let all of these terrible things happen to me? Even though I did not verbally voice these thoughts directly to God they were in my heart and my anger started showing up in my rebellious behavior. 1 Kings 8:39 says, *"Since you know his heart (for you alone know the hearts of all men)"*. God knew everything I was feeling inside toward Him but He never stopped loving me. *"You know my when I sit and when I rise; you perceive my thoughts from afar."* (Psalm 139:2) How grateful I am for God's longsuffering mercy and compassion toward me or I would have been destroyed! *"Yet he was merciful; he forgave their iniquities and did not destroy them. Time after time he restrained his anger and did not stir up his full wrath. He remembered that they were but flesh".* (Psalm 78:38-39)

My second big mistake that would lead me into a season of ungodly living was in not **being careful** in my choice of new friends. I chose people who were not Christians and they lived their lives to satisfy the flesh not the spirit. Due to my choice of new friends I slowly got sucked into the bar scene and drinking on a pretty regular basis. Psalm 141:4 says, *"Let not my heart be drawn to what is evil, to take part in wicked deeds with men who are evildoers; let me not eat of their delicacies."* It seemed like a good idea at the time because I could not stand the loneliness at home and after all, I told myself, it was a possible way to meet new 'prince' prospects. I knew he was out there I just needed to get out and find him! I wanted so badly to meet **"Mr. Right"** but my problem was I wanted **"Mr. Right NOW"**!

At first, I knew clearly, that everything I was doing was wrong and I felt the conviction of the Spirit but still I continued in my rebellious ways anyway because of my anger and pain. Was I truly born again, had I really accepted Christ as my Savior? **Absolutely**, I know I was but I was so crippled by the pain of my insecurities that I was not able to walk in victory very long before I fell into sin again. It seemed that the more I ignored the warnings of the Holy Spirit the more miserable I became. Galatians 5:16-17 says, *"So I say, live by the Spirit, and you will not gratify the desires of the sinful nature. For the sinful nature desires what is contrary to the Spirit and the Spirit what is contrary to the sinful nature. They are in conflict with each other, so that you do not do what you want."* I would repent but then fall back into the same traps of Satan again and again because of the terrible bondage that had wound itself tightly around me. Romans 7:18-20 describes exactly how I felt: *"I know that nothing good lives in me, that is, in my sinful nature. For I have the desire to do what is good, but I cannot* *carry it out. For what I do is not the good I want to do; no, the evil I do not want to do—this I keep on doing. Now if I do what I do not want to do, it is no longer I who do it, but it is sin living in me that does it."* There was a war of **good** and **evil** ragging inside of me and I just wanted peace and quiet but I was looking for it in **all the wrong faces and places**. I just wanted to tell all the voices yelling inside me *"will everyone please sit down and shut up"*! I needed some peace and quiet but I was totally going in the wrong direction to find it.

Over the next four years even though I never married again, I was involved in several serious relationships that broke my heart. Because of two of these relationships, twice I again attempted suicide, once by over the counter sleeping pills and once with a hose attached to the tail pipe of my car. The combination of antidepressants and the alcohol I drank I believe were a deadly combination for me. It says clearly on the prescription instructions not to drink alcohol while taking the antidepressants but I did not pay attention to the warning. I only drank at night and on the week-ends but I was also slowly increasing the amount of alcohol I was drinking to numb my pain. Alcohol was an **instant fix** for my pain but it was always there again when the numbness wore off. Alcohol seemed to give me the confidence I so badly lacked. Even though I had witnessed first hand from my mother and sister how alcohol **could destroy your life** it did not seem to deter me from drinking. I drove home very intoxicated on several occasions without ever considering the danger to others or to me and thankfully God sent his angels to protect me and the others in my path. *"For he will command his angels concerning you to guard you in all your ways."* (Psalm 91:11) Did I deserve God's protection—**NO**, but deep in my heart, even in my pain, I loved the LORD and He knew my heart. *"'Because he loves* *me, says the LORD, I will rescue him; I will protect him, for he acknowledges my name. He will call upon me, and I will answer him; I will be with him in trouble, I will deliver him and honor him.'"* (Psalm 91:14-15) I was in deep trouble emotionally and spiritually and needed His protection.

The first of the next two suicide attempts occurred about a year after I moved back to Florence. I **constantly** thought of suicide every time something went wrong in my life that I did not know how to handle, especially after broken relationships. The thought of suicide to solve your problems were *haunting echoes of my past, words I had heard my mother say many times*. The LORD was compassionate and merciful and once again rescued me in each of these attempts and saved my life. I was so needy for love that I fell hard in my relationships and when they ended, I was devastated. After this particular break up I decided to throw a huge 'pity party' for myself. I bought a large bottle of wine and proceeded to drink away my sorrows. I kept drinking for several hours and apparently out drank myself! All that I remember is waking up at around 4:30 a.m. and trying to sit up and I could not move. I know now that the LORD woke me up because I would never have been able to wake up on my own; I was in such a deep sleep. My body felt like it had turned into four thousand pounds of lead. I could hardly move my legs they were so heavy. I was so disoriented and did not remember that I had taken any pills. I thought that I might have had a stroke or something. I continued to try to sit up and finally was able to move enough to swing my legs over the side of the bed. I looked at the clock and then tried to remember what happened. Thankfully, to this day I have no memory of taking the pills or going upstairs and putting myself to bed that night. I felt very strange and my brain was extremely foggy. I could not stand up and so I got down on my hands and knees and managed to crawl to my bathroom. I thought I was having a nightmare at first but then I realized I was awake. My mouth was extremely dry so I drank some water. Then a **horrible sinking feeling** came over me in the pit of my stomach that something really bad was wrong with me and that *I* had done something terrible to cause it. I remember crying out loud, "Oh my God, what have I done?" *"Our God is a God who saves; from the Sovereign LORD comes escape from death."* (Psalm 68:19)

I realized I needed to go downstairs and see if I could figure out what I had done. Somehow I managed to go down the stairs on my behind because I still could not walk. When I got to the living room I looked around to see if what I thought I had done was true. There on the coffee table was the empty bottle of pills and half empty bottle of wine. Then I knew this was not a nightmare but reality— I had once again taken an overdose. I crawled to the kitchen to get some milk to drink, thinking it would help my stomach somehow and neutralize the drugs. Then I realized I needed to call someone to come and take me to the hospital.

I felt so strange, *like I was dying*, my life was slipping away from me and I really did not want to die! I told my girlfriend I was scared to death and to please hurry and come to get me. We went to the hospital and they made me drink some horrible tasting charcoal mixture to neutralize the drugs but they did not pump my stomach like the first time. I told them I had been drinking a lot and that I did not remember taking the pills and so they let me go home and did not keep me in the psych ward like last time either. I was so glad they did not keep me in the hospital. I know that this too was because the LORD was watching over me and He knew I could not handle that again. I also did not have any health insurance and I would not have been able to pay the bills for an extended hospital stay.

Even after this suicide attempt I continued to look for someone to love me because of my terrible insecurity and brokenness that had now developed into gigantic proportions. Even though I had received healing from my father's death, I still needed to believe that I was worth loving and I just kept coming up short. I had become extremely vulnerable to the slightest amount of attention from anyone and probably gave my heart away much too quickly. It became a vicious cycle like a whirlpool that sucked me into its grasps and then dragged me down into the darkness only to spit me out again on the shore of loneliness. My heart kept crying *"why won't someone just love me and not leave me this time"*. What is wrong with me? I wanted to know where that 'prince charming' was and what was taking him so long to find me?

My second attempt at suicide was a couple of years later in 2003 after another break up with someone that I had fallen in love with. I truly believed this man was my 'soul mate' out of all the men I have married or dated. He was kind and not dysfunctional like all my other choices. We had so much in common and could even finish each others thoughts and sentences. We just seemed to fit together like a hand in a glove. There was a group of us that went to happy hour each week after work and I met him in this group of people. He was married but separating to get a divorce—or so he said at the time. I knew better than to get involved with someone who was not yet divorced because I had been hurt by this kind of situation before. I also knew that according to what God thought about the situation it was considered adultery because he was not divorced. I did not pay attention to what the Spirit was trying to tell me because I wanted things my way. Finally, I had found someone who thought I was beautiful and desired me. I was ecstatic and I was going to get my "fairy tale ending this time"!

He called me beautiful all of the time and oh, my goodness he was a champion among princes at saying all the things I needed to hear. I just knew this 'prince' was really going to work out this time! *Oh, if I just had a dollar for every time that thought has crossed my mind I would be in the Fortune 500 Club by now!*

I can see now, as I look back that God had already started putting Christian people in my path to bring me back to repentance and a close relationship with Him but I was still angry at Him. I wanted my flesh to feel better, even though all of the things I had been doing was only making me feel worse! *"The mind of sinful man is death, but the mind controlled by the Spirit is life and peace."* (Romans 8:6) I was letting my sinful nature control my mind and I was full of turmoil and death. Colossians 3:5 says, *"Put to death, therefore, whatever belongs to your earthly nature: sexual immorality, impurity, lust, evil desires and greed, which is idolatry."* I think those pretty much cover all of the results that were coming forth from my giving in to my earthly nature! I was trying to put a man in the place that only God can fill and that is idolatry in every sense of the word and our God is a **jealous God**. *"He is a holy God; he is a jealous God."* (Joshua 24:19)

Even in my sinful waywardness, deep down inside because the Holy Spirit lived in me, I knew what I was doing was wrong. *"But when he, the Spirit of truth, comes, he will guide you into all truth."* (John 16:13) I finally told this man that until he was divorced I could not continue with this relationship. He kept postponing the separation proceedings and finally decided not to divorce because of his children. I knew the divorce was not going to happen and I could not live as 'the other woman'. It was a *whirlwind romance* (from start to finish) that swept me off my feet but the after effects left miles of scattered debris that would take some time to clean up. I believe I had truly fallen in love with him, in a way I never had before and the loss would take me a long time to get over. One more time, I had loved and lost. Like so many times before someone else came before me, his children, and I was not worth the fight.

Once again, I threw myself another 'pity party', proceeded to drink a big bottle of wine to get up the courage to end my life. After drinking quite a lot and taking a prescription sleeping pill I hooked a garden hose to my car's tail pipe and ran it into the car through the back window. I decided the pills were not doing the job very well so I would try **something different** this time. I owned a .380 revolver but I was too afraid to use it—that would leave too big a mess and so I decided on carbon monoxide poisoning. I wanted out of the pain but I was more terrified of a violent type of death. I just wanted to fall asleep quietly and wake up on the other side where there was no more emotional pain. I don't really remember what happened after I sat in the car only that my attempt was unsuccessful, *I gave up and went back inside my apartment alive—but still in pain.*

I feel that I must address the issue here as to whether or not I would have gone to Heaven had I succeeded in a suicide attempt. I know there are many who will disagree with my belief that I would indeed have gone to Heaven if I had committed suicide. I was genuinely born again, Christ was my Savior, and I do believe with all of my heart that if I had succeeded in ending my life I would still have gone to Heaven. Romans 8:38 says, *"for I am convinced that neither death nor life, neither angels nor demons, neither the present nor the future, nor any powers, neither height nor depth, nor anything else in all creation, will be able to separate us from the love of God that is in Christ Jesus our Lord."* Romans 8:35 also tells us that nothing shall separate us from the love of Christ. I knew and loved Jesus but I was in so much pain emotionally that I was not capable of thinking clearly. Deep down in my heart I really did not want to die; I just wanted the pain and darkness to stop! God knew my heart and my pain. *"Nothing in all creation is hidden from God's sight."* (Hebrews 4:13) Suicide is always a cry for help, the LORD heard my cries and He will hear yours too. *"Before they call I will answer; while they are still speaking I will hear".* (Isaiah 66:24) I wanted the dreadful pain that was suffocating me to end and suicide seemed to be the only way. Satan of course was only too happy to reinforce my belief that suicide was the best answer because he is always out to kill, steal or destroy us. (John 10:10) But Praise God, Jesus has defeated Satan and his kingdom of darkness. *"And having disarmed the powers and authorities, he made a public spectacle of them, triumphing over them by the cross."* (Colossians 2:15)

    Jesus really did understand my dark pain because He too has walked through a valley of great darkness and sorrow. On the night before His death in the Garden of Gethsemane, He was in so much agony that He sweat drops of blood. Listen to the words from Matthew 26:38, *"Then he said to them, 'My soul is overwhelmed with sorrow to the point of death'"*. In Luke 22:44 it says, *"And being in anguish, he prayed more earnestly, and his sweat was like drops of blood falling to the ground."* I did not sweat drops of blood but my soul was overwhelmed with sorrow to the point of wanting to die. Hebrews 4:15 says, *"For we do not have a high priest who is unable to sympathize with our weaknesses, but we have one who has been tempted in every way, just as we are—yet was without sin."* Tragically I once again had tried to end my pain-filled life but thank you Jesus—the hose idea didn't work either!

I had gone back to work as a legal secretary in 2002 because I was too afraid to trust the LORD to stay at home and paint full time. I was making $31,000 a year in my office job and had lots of portraits to paint as well. I should have been very thankful and content with my life but I was still miserable on the inside. I decided I wanted to buy a house because I was tired of wasting my money by renting—**bigger shopping**! Even though I did not have enough credit for the approval of my loan I continued to push ahead to buy a house that was way too expensive for me. Eventually I worked out a deal with a home owner to 'lease-to-own' their house for a year and that would build up enough credit for my loan. I was stubborn and full of pride, not willing to listen to anyone or see the signs the LORD was trying to show me—I should wait.

While I was in the process of buying the house my blood pressure shot up one day at work to 195 over 105. There was a lot of stress involved with my legal job. The onset of menopausal symptoms and my spiritual turmoil inside also were contributing factors to my blood pressure attack. When I went to the doctor, he told me I had been close to having a stroke or "red lining" as he called it and I needed to find a job that involved less stress. Instead of changing my decision about the house, I forged ahead anyway and started moving into the house. I decided I would just quit my job and paint full time because I had twelve portraits to paint. My thinking was terribly clouded and unrealistic because I had just obligated myself to lease payments of $850.00 a month and now I was quitting my steady job. *Actually, I wasn't thinking at all!* I was in way over my head but I could not see it! I was too busy being proud of the fact that I was buying a house to realize I could not afford it. *"Why do you boast of your valleys, boast of your valleys so fruitful? O unfaithful daughter, you trust in your riches and say, 'Who will attack me?'"* (Jeremiah 49:4)

As I look back now I am amazed at my **arrogance** and **stupidity** in my decision about the purchase of the house. After about four months the portrait work began to run out. I had not had any calls for more work and so I knew I had to go back to work again in an office job. I worked in a couple of part time jobs until I was finally offered another full time job in legal work again. Even through all of my stupidity **God was faithful** and provided the finances for my bills. I did not want to go back to work in the legal field because I knew the stress was too much for me but I did not have any choice. My art was not succeeding enough to support me so I felt I had no other choice. I also had to "eat crow" and admit my mistake about buying the house! Pride had come to me and so had the fall! *"Pride goes before destruction, a haughty spirit before a fall."* (Proverbs 16:18) I had to break the lease, forfeit the $2,000.00 down payment money (which I had borrowed) and move back into an apartment once again. *I had to step out of the fantasy world I was living in and climb down off of the high horse I had been riding.* I was humiliated, ashamed and felt like such a failure again! My world was crumbling down around me but *God was still in control* and he was teaching me Humility 101 which brings wisdom. I did not possess an ounce of **humility** or **wisdom**! *"When pride comes, then comes disgrace, but with humility comes wisdom."* (Proverbs 11:2)

During all of this time my menopause symptoms were steadily getting worse and so did the depression that had set in again. Before I moved out of the house I was struggling terribly to function because of the depression. Suicide was in the forefront of my mind daily and so one morning (before I started working part time) I decided I could not go on anymore. I had failed miserably with my decision about the house and now I was going to have to move again and I just could not do it. Even though I was terribly worried about who would take care of my two cats and my bird I just could not take anymore. My pets had always been my best friends ever since I was a little girl. *They were the only ones that were always there with me when I felt alone. They had been my only source of unconditional love since I was a little girl.* I never really considered how my daughter would feel because we were still not very close. I had failed her as a mother too and I really did not think she would miss me because she had her daddy and they were very close. I guess I did not think anyone would care if I was gone because of my low self-esteem.

Suicide would be the easiest way to end it all so I went and got my revolver and went in the bathroom. I thought it would not be as hard to clean up the mess if I shot myself in the tub. I laid down on the floor and started sobbing uncontrollably and crying aloud to the LORD. *"The cords of death entangled me; the torrents of destruction overwhelmed me. The cords of the grave coiled around me; the snares of death confronted me. In my distress I called to the LORD; I cried to my God for help. From his temple he heard my voice; my cry came before him into his ears."* (Psalm 18:4-6) I lay there for a long time trying to get up the nerve to pull the trigger and **suddenly** my door bell rang downstairs. **Once again** the LORD had rescued me, he sent a friend of mine by to check on me and her visit stopped my suicide attempt. *"The LORD will keep you from all harm—he will watch over your life; the LORD will watch over your coming and going both now and forevermore."* (Psalm 121:7-8)

That would be the *last time* I would **EVER** attempt or even **think** about suicide again! A day or two after this incident I heard the LORD very clearly in my spirit tell me, *"You need to* *stop taking those antidepressants because they are making you worse."* I was too afraid right then to be obedient to His voice and stop taking them. My reasoning was if I felt this way about suicide while I was taking the antidepressants then I would be **even worse** if I stopped taking them. They were supposed to be preventing the depression and yet I was **still suicidal**. I just did not understand at the time that they were actually causing me to think more about suicide! So I continued to take them for about nine more months and during that time the doctor actually doubled my dosage thinking I was not taking a high enough dosage. He also started giving me heavy doses of estrogen to try and control my menopause symptoms and the combination of the two drove me over the edge. Emotionally I was a walking nightmare!

I was so miserable with myself and everything in my life! I hated the job where I worked because it was legal work again; it was something God had not gifted me to do. I know I must have made the people I worked with miserable too because I was so miserable. I frequently had to call in sick because I was not sleeping **at all** during the night and by morning I was exhausted. I came home every night after work and would drink a couple of strong drinks and go to bed so I would not have to think about how miserable my life was. However, I was still determined in my search for my 'prince charming' in the midst of all my misery but without much luck. I decided to try the internet dating services because everyone else seemed to be having luck with them and besides there were "no descent single men" in Florence that I could find. I thought maybe the match dating sites could broaden my search and I wanted to move away from Florence anyway because there were too many painful memories here for me now. I thought if I moved somewhere else, I could be happy, I just did not realize yet that the happiness needed to come from the inside. *Unless I was happy right where I was I would never be happy anywhere else!*

God knew exactly what I needed and was orchestrating all the events in my life so that He could start my healing symphony! I was running hard from my pain straight into the Father's loving arms. I was the prodigal daughter who needed to come to her senses and return home to the Father's tender care. *"When he came to his senses, he said, How many of my father's hired men have food to spare, and here I am starving to death! I will set out and go back to my father and say to him: Father, I have sinned against heaven and against you. I am no longer worthy to be called your son; make me like one of your hired men."* (Luke 15:17-19) My Father would be standing there waiting with open arms to welcome me home like so many times before. *"But while he was still a long way off, his father saw him and was filled with compassion for him; he ran to his son, threw his arms around him and kissed him."* (Luke 15:20)

> *"I will heal their waywardness and love them freely, for my anger has turned away from them."*
> *Hosea 14:4*

Chapter 8

The Last Straw

"They reeled and staggered like drunken men; they were at their wits' end. Then they cried out to the LORD in their trouble, and he brought them out of their distress."
Psalm 107:27-28

September 10, 2004 started out just like any other miserable day in my life but it was going to end in victory for God's Kingdom. I was so physically sick by this time from the antidepressants and estrogen I was taking that I could barely walk from my bedroom to the bathroom without being out of breath. I knew something had to give because I could not go on much longer the way I was feeling. Events were set in motion that day that could have destroyed my life if I had given in to them as I had in the past.

It was a Friday and my day to have half of the afternoon off. I was getting ready to leave for the day and my boss called me into his office to talk. He told me he was going to have to let me go because the job was not working out and that he did not feel I had learned the job as well as he had hoped. **WHAT did he**

just say? *I could not believe my ears!* Even though I was doing a different type of legal work from my previous experience I thought that I was doing well under the circumstances. I just sat there in shock! I had known this man for a long time and I could not believe he was doing this to me. He told me he was going to give me two weeks severance pay and I remember thinking, *"what in the world am I going to do"*. I did have a couple of portraits to paint but what would happen then. I had never been fired from a job before and I was **humiliated**. I was also confused because I knew my work was not behind or anything. The tears started to fall silently down my cheeks and I said to him, *"well that's it; this is the straw that is going to break the camel's back!"* I did not know at the time what a prophetic statement that was!

I gathered up my things and left the office still stunned by what just happened. *What in the world was I supposed to do now? How much more could I stand?* I was truly at the end of my rope, knocked flat on my face with despair but right where the LORD could now help me. With tears streaming down my face I went by my bank to deposit my last paycheck and then drove home in a trance trying to figure out what I was going to do next.

When I got home I sat down on the chair weeping in disbelief with waves of fear washing over me. I cried out in desperation to the LORD seeking answers from the only person I knew that could help me. Instead of asking Him "why" this time as I always did in the past, I just asked Him *"what LORD, what are you trying to show me?"* I believe this made all the difference in the final outcome of my healing and deliverance. I was at a turning point in my life now—*I could do it my way or God's*, **it was my choice**. Everything I had trusted in came suddenly crashing down around me. *"This sin will become for* *you like a high wall, cracked and bulging, that collapses suddenly, in an instant. It will break in pieces like pottery, shattered so mercilessly that among its pieces not a fragment will be found for taking coals from a hearth or scooping water out of a cistern."* (Isaiah 30:14-15) Instead of having a "pity party" and being angry with God, which was my normal way of reacting in the past, I decided to ask for God's help. I knew God was the only one who could help me now and for a change, I was all ears for His suggestions and solutions to my predicament. I was ready to cooperate with Him this time because I had tried everything else and failed.

The memory of all my sins and wild living flooded in like a tidal wave and I cried out to Jesus for forgiveness. I had finally come to the end of myself and this was the place that God could start my intensive healing journey. The straw **had broken** the camel's back and I was lying flat out in the **burning sand of despair**! In a time that looked so dark God would begin to shed His light and show me the way. *"I will lead the blind by ways they have not known, along unfamiliar paths I will guide them; I will turn the darkness into light before them and make the rough places smooth. These are the things I will do; I will not forsake them."* (Isaiah 42:16)

On the same day I was fired I got busy and started looking for jobs on the Florence and Charleston newspaper websites. Over the next few days and weeks I began to seek the LORD'S will for my life. I needed answers to my many questions about my life. Should I move to Charleston where I had wanted to live for some time? Should I look for another office job or some other type of work? Should I stay home and paint full time? People were always telling me I should be painting full time and not working as a secretary in an office. I started sending resumes for creative decorating jobs listed in the Charleston and

Florence paper. I decided since I was good with colors and decorating maybe I could find a creative job instead of secretarial work. I was still so sick physically though I did not think I was able to go back to work in an office or to move out of town but I continued to send the resumes anyway. According to God's Word I prayed that the LORD would open any door that He would have me to walk through and close all doors that were not His will. *"What he opens no one can shut, and what he shuts no one can open."* (Revelation 3:7)

I **finally** followed the LORD'S previous instructions to me and *stopped taking the antidepressants*. I had been living consistently on antidepressants for seven years. I started using natural herbs for my depression and menopause symptoms. I was determined to get well and I did not want to take any more prescription medication because of the terrible side effects they caused. My body ached all over from the effects of the estrogen overload and I had symptoms of fibromyalgia and autoimmune deficiency syndrome.

The first two weeks after I stopped taking my antidepressants I was so dizzy I had to stay in my house and not drive my vehicle. The LORD led me to a wonderful woman named Mary who worked in a local natural health store and He has used her over the past three years to help heal me physically. During these three years, I have not gone back to a doctor but have relied on the LORD to be my Jehovah-rapha, "the LORD who healeth" (Exodus 15:26), my healer and He has been faithful.

Although I was scared to death to stop taking the antidepressants and the withdrawal was painful at first, I can see now that it was **absolutely necessary** for my survival. I obeyed God's instruction and **He has been faithful!** Psalm 91:14 says, *"'Because he loves me,' says the Lord, I will rescue* *him; I will protect him, for he acknowledges my name."* Surely, the Lord has rescued and protected this wounded woman who loves Him and acknowledges His name! I have not suffered from depression and not once have I even thought about suicide since I stopped taking the prescription antidepressant! If I feel myself becoming a little down from time to time, then I take some natural herbs that raise my serotonin levels and the depression is lifted. **Oh Praise His Holy name!** One of the first verses the LORD gave me in 2004 to claim as a promise from Him is Jeremiah 30:17 that says, *"'But I will restore you to health and heal your wounds', declares the LORD."* **He has been faithful to both!**

Some time in late October of 2004, I received a phone call about a job interview with a decorating store in Charleston. I was not sure whether I should even drive down there for the interview because I did not know if I was financially or physically able to move. My God has such a wonderful sense of humor! I remember laying there in the bed the morning of the interview talking, **no arguing** with the LORD and saying there is no way I can move to Charleston right now, I'm too sick and anyway I don't have the finances to move either. I heard the LORD almost in a laughing reply say to me in a gentle whisper in my spirit, "Listen, if I can get two million Israelites packed up with everything they needed and moved out of Egypt, I think I could get you moved to Charleston"! I started laughing because I knew He was right and so I got up, got dressed and drove to Charleston for the interview.

On my way to Charleston just a few miles from my house on my way out of town, an **amazing** thing happened. I looked up through my windshield as I was driving and there directly above my car was the **most incredible** *American eagle soaring in a circle.* He was flying so low that I could see the white tips on his wings and the gold color of his beak and feet. It took my breath away he was so beautiful and majestic! Immediately the verse came to my mind, *"but those who wait on the LORD will renew their strength, they will soar on wings like eagles; they will run and not grow weary, they will walk and not faint."* (Isaiah 40:31) Then I also remembered, *"He will cover you with his feathers, and under his wings you will find refuge; his faithfulness will be your shield and rampart."* (Psalm 91:4) I knew the LORD had sent that eagle above me at that precise moment to let me know He was watching over me and protecting me and that if I would just wait on His timing everything would be okay and I would grow strong again. This was to be the first of many times the LORD would use nature's birds to show me His presence was with me sheltering and guiding me on my healing journey.

I was offered the job in Charleston that day but I did not accept the job. The salary they offered was much too low for me to be able to live in Charleston and I knew I needed to wait on the LORD'S timing. As much as I wanted to move to Charleston I needed to learn to use some wisdom in my decision making skills and not just jump out blindly as I had done in the past. I am sure you are asking as I did, "well, why did the LORD have me go to the interview if I was not supposed to accept the job". I believe it was one of the tests from the LORD to see if I would be obedient and trust Him even when the outcome was not what I wanted. He was telling me He could move me *even if things looked impossible* but I needed to wait on His timing and plan.

In the beginning days of my time at home, many times I got down on the floor, laid flat on my face and cried out to the LORD asking for His forgiveness of all my many terrible sins. I was **genuinely sorry** for my sins and in **true repentance** I was changing my previous life style. Acts 3:19 says, *"Repent, then, and turn to God, so that your sins may be wiped out, that times of refreshing may come from the LORD."* Many of my changes were immediate! The cursing that had come out of my mouth so frequently with such ease ceased instantly and I did not want or feel the need to drink alcohol excessively anymore. I started to see the dangers in it for me, especially in light of the devastating effects I witnessed in my mother and sister's life. In the beginning I continued to drink a glass of wine now and then at night to calm my anxiety inside but now I don't need it anymore. I have learned to run to the LORD if I become anxious or fearful and He calms my fears like He did the stormy waters of the Sea of Galilee. *"And he arose, and rebuked the wind, and said unto the sea, Peace, be still. And the wind ceased, and there was a great calm."* (Mark 4:39) **Jesus is the best anxiety pill you can ever take!** *"Do not be anxious about anything, but in everything, by prayer and petition, with thanksgiving, present your requests to God."* (Philippians 4:6) When I keep my mind focused on Him then He keeps me calm. *"Thou wilt keep **him** in perfect peace, whose mind is stayed on thee, because he trusteth in thee."* (Isaiah 26:3)

I was genuinely heartsick over the life I had lived the past four years and I just could not believe I had fallen so far into sin. I could not seem to get past my sinfulness and accept the LORD'S forgiveness even though it tells us in 1 John 1:9, *"if we confess our sins, he is faithful and just and will forgive us our sins and purify us from all unrighteousness."* I knew the Word of God told me I was forgiven by God but I was having a hard time forgiving myself for my failures. Jesus' death had washed me white as snow but Satan was continually reminding me of my filthy rags! The voices in my head of my past sins were screaming my unworthiness of Jesus' forgiveness. *"'Come now, let us reason together,' says the LORD. 'Though your sins are like scarlet, they shall be as white as snow; though they are red as crimson, they shall be like wool."* (Isaiah 1:18)

I constantly kept asking myself how a once **godly** person could do such **ungodly** things. How could the LORD possibly forgive me and accept me back as one of His own when I had strayed so far and fallen so deeply into sin? Satan was in hot pursuit of me now that I had rededicated my life to God and was returning to a life of holiness. He was continuously reminding me of each and every one of my terrible sins and telling me that God could not possibly want me back! I would confront Satan with the Word of God and tell him what my Father said about my sins and he would leave me alone for a while. *"As far as the east is from the west, so far has he removed our transgressions from us."* (Psalm 103:12) Satan is the accuser of the brethren and he had shifted into "turbo gear" with his accusations against me. *"Then he showed me Joshua the high priest standing before the angel of the LORD, and Satan standing at his right side to accuse him."* (Zechariah 3:1) Again in Revelation 12:10 it says of Satan, *"For the accuser of the brothers, who accuses them before our God day and night, has been hurled down."* I can tell you he was **furious** and literally accusing me **day** and **night**!

Early one morning I received the answer to my question **if** God really had accepted me back and forgiven me. As I lay in bed I turned on the radio and listened to a pastor tell a beautiful story of how a shepherd cures a lamb that wanders. The shepherd breaks one of the lamb's legs, then wraps and sets the broken leg. He puts the lamb on his shoulders and keeps him close to him until the leg has mended. Once he puts the lamb down again the lamb **never wanders away from the shepherd again**! Ever so gently, I heard the LORD tell me, *"that's what*

*I have done with you my lamb and when you **are healed** you will never wander away from me again."* I started crying then, and even now as I think back on the sweet tenderness of the moment. I was then able to accept the circumstances in my life as being from the hand of the LORD. **He** had broken my legs and now **He** was going to keep me **close** to **Him** until my brokenness was healed. *"He who scattered Israel will gather them and watch over his flock like a shepherd."* (Jeremiah 31:10) Listen to the tender words of Jesus in Luke 15:4-6 about a lost sheep that is found, *"Suppose one of you has a hundred sheep and loses one of them. Does he not leave the ninety-nine in the open country and go after the lost sheep until he finds it? And when he finds it, he joyfully puts it on his shoulders and goes home. Then he calls his friends and neighbors together and says, 'Rejoice with me; I have found my lost sheep.'* My Shepherd had put me on His shoulders and Heaven was rejoicing! *"I tell you that in the same way there will be more rejoicing in heaven over one sinner who repents than over ninety-nine righteous persons who do not need to repent."* (Luke 15:7) I knew that until my wounds were healed there was nowhere I would rather be than on my Shepherd's strong shoulders where I would be **safe**. *"Let the beloved of the LORD rest secure in him, for he shields him all day long, and the one the LORD loves rests between his shoulders."* (Deuteronomy 33:12)

    I started visiting different churches in Florence looking for a church home soon after I was fired. I was not able to go every Sunday because I was still so sick physically. Most Sundays, I would stay home in bed and just spend precious quiet time alone with the LORD reading His Word. I started watching Christian shows almost continually every day. During those first few months I was not able to stand up or sit down for long periods due to the soreness in my muscles and back. I also started attending a weekly women's Bible Study to hear the Word of God and fellowship with other believers. I eventually started attending a prayer service during the week in a small church with one of my friends. I was still a wreck emotionally, as well as physically, but being around other believers who prayed helped me tremendously. Even though I still suffered from anxiety and fear, deep down inside of me there was *a peace that was as still as glass.* I had again found the peace that passes all understanding that can only come from the LORD. *"Thou will keep **him** in perfect peace, **whose** mind is stayed **on thee**, because he trusteth in thee."* (Isaiah 26:4 KJV) My mind was constantly thinking about the LORD and His Word every waking hour because that was the only way I could survive and the result was **perfect peace**. *"And the peace of God, which transcends all understanding, will guard your hearts and your minds in Christ Jesus."* (Philippians 4:7)

In February of 2005, I became deeply troubled again about my prior sinfulness and the state of my salvation. I could not seem to let go of my sinful past and believe *I was truly forgiven.* Thanks to Satan and his whispering lies, I started to doubt whether I had ever truly been saved. I was on my way to prayer service late one afternoon around 6:00 when I decided to go by my bank to deposit my unemployment check. As I was driving, I was watching the beautiful colors in the sky as the sun was setting. It had been cloudy and dreary for most of the day but it was clearing off now and there were just a few patches of dark blue clouds along the horizon near the sun. The sky was an artist's dream sunset painted with changing colors of vibrant lavenders, luminous pinks and glowing oranges. As I drove through a large parking lot near my bank I looked up at the sky and suddenly there appeared in the dark blue clouds near the horizon the shape of a huge angel standing and blowing a trumpet. I stared at it for several seconds thinking **"wow, that's unusual"**. I think I even thought "is it time for the rapture and the angel is getting ready to blow the trumpet to call us home"! All of a sudden out of nowhere, a **huge perfectly formed brilliant red crimson cross** appeared beside the angel in the clouds. I was so stunned that I immediately stopped my car in the middle of the parking lot to stare at the sky. I blinked my eyes a couple of times to see if I was *'hallucinating or something'* but the red cross was still there and remained in the sky for several minutes. It was an awesome sight to see! My eyes filled with tears as my heart was flooded with love at the memory of the words Jesus spoke from the cross, ***"It is finished"*** (John 19:30). The work was done on the cross and I was redeemed! **Never again** would I doubt my salvation or His forgiveness of my sins. God went out of His way to paint me a vivid picture in the sky that day and reassure me of my soul's condition—**covered by the blood of the cross.** *"And, having made peace through the blood of his cross, by him to reconcile all things unto himself—by him, I say, whether they be things in earth, or things in heaven."* (Colossians 1:20 KJV) I was seeking answers concerning my salvation and the LORD was gracious and compassionate toward me. *"The LORD longs to be gracious to you; he rises to show you compassion. For the LORD is a God of justice. Blessed are all who wait for him!"* (Isaiah 30:18) Oh, was I ever blessed by that sight in the sky!

I remember thinking to myself when I first saw the cross, *"oh I wish I had a camera to take a picture of this"* not remembering that I had a camera on my cell phone. It was a new cell phone and I think I was so flabbergasted by the whole event that I did not think about the camera being on the phone! I wanted someone else to witness this **"amazing phenomenon"** and also to reassure me that it was really there in the sky so I called my girlfriend who went to the little church I was attending. She worked across the street from the parking lot where I was and so I called her on my cell phone (the one with the camera on it!) and told her to go outside and look at the sunset because there was a huge red cross in the sky. She went outside to look but there was a tree line blocking her view and she could not see the horizon. When I got to Church I also asked several people if they had seen the huge red cross in the sky but no one else had witnessed it. It was meant for my eyes only as a sign from the LORD that I was indeed His child. Even now as I remember that day I am still in awe of what I saw and the **great lengths** that the LORD will go to show us **His love for us**! Our mighty God loves to show off and I guess because I am an artist and a very visual person He just loves painting up there in the sky for me! Paint on sweet Father, may your wonders never cease! *"He is your praise; he is your God, who performed for you those great and awesome wonders you saw with your own eyes."* (Deuteronomy 10:21) Heaven's angel was blowing a trumpet that afternoon and announcing that I had been to the foot of the blood red cross of Calvary and Jesus was mine. This was not going to be the last masterpiece the LORD painted in the sky for me. The next one would come in the same month exactly a year later in 2006.

Months passed and during my time of waiting on the LORD to show me what I was to do I continually read the Word of God and listened non-stop 24/7 to Christian radio and televisions programs. If there is one thing that I could put my finger on that **I know** healed me over the past three years it is the continual input of **God's Word** into my spirit through either my eyes or ears. I was constantly feeding on His Word for strength and healing. God's Word has nourished my spirit the way an IV of fluids feeds a dehydrated body. There was no miraculous flash of light from Heaven but just the constant reading of the Word of God that increased my faith and my faith healed me. Not only did I study His Word but I believed and obeyed its truths. *"So, then, faith **cometh** by hearing, and hearing by the word of God."* (Romans 10:17) In order to change my old sinful pattern of thinking like the world I needed to renew my mind with the Word of God. *"Do not conform any longer to the pattern of this world, but be transformed by the renewing of your mind. Then you will be able to test and approve what God's will is—his good, pleasing and perfect will."* (Romans 12:2) I knew that I had to turn away from all of my old ways and live according to God's Word if there was going to be any hope of climbing out of the pits I had been living in. God's Word transformed my life through all of the ways listed in 2 Timothy 3:16-17. It says, *"All scripture is God-breathed and is useful for teaching, rebuking, correcting and training in righteousness, so that the man of God may be thoroughly equipped for every good work."* The LORD was using His Word to equip me for the good living instead of the life I had been living. Psalm 119:37 says what my heart was feeling, *"turn my eyes away from worthless things; preserve my life according to your word."*

Not long after I first saw the statue in the cemetery, I felt the LORD leading me to paint a picture of Jesus and the Woman at the Well. I decided soon after I first started staying home full time that it was time to start the painting. One Sunday I decided to ride to the cemetery and take pictures of the statue to use as a reference in my painting. I started the painting several weeks later and continued to work on it off and on over the next months. I had seen a couple of paintings of the woman at the well but I felt the LORD leading me to paint mine with a deeper spiritual meaning. He wanted me to paint water coming out of

Jesus' hand and flowing into the well to show vividly that He is **"the living water"**. At first, I really did not know how the LORD wanted to use the painting but I just knew He wanted me to paint it. Then when the LORD laid it on my heart to write this book and tell my story of healing I realized that the painting could be used for the cover of my book. Months went by and I would not touch the painting because I had a hard time working on it. It was such a personal part of my life's story and there were many painful memories involved with each stroke. In a way that I cannot explain the LORD used my work on the painting as another one of His healing tools in my life. *"As the heavens are higher than the earth, so are my ways higher than your ways and my thoughts than your thoughts."* (Isaiah 55:9) It has taken me two years to complete the painting but Praise God I finally finished it in June of 2007! Thank you Father, for each stroke of the brush that helped to **"paint me well"**!

I prayed for God to help me overcome my past defeats and He answered by giving me a voracious appetite for His Word. *"He sent forth his word and healed them; he rescued them from the grave."* (Psalm 107:20) I have always loved studying God's Word but during my season of sin that love had grown cold. I needed victory this time if I was going to survive and *I was tired of living a defeated life*. Therefore, I diligently searched the scriptures for the answers I needed. God's Word watered the dry and parched places in my soul and became a **fountain of life** to me. *"You are a garden fountain, a well of flowing water streaming down from Lebanon."* (Song of Songs 4:15) *"Water will gush forth in the wilderness and streams in the desert. The burning sand will become a pool, the thirsty ground bubbling springs."* (Isaiah 35:6-7) I was thirsty to know that I was loved and He filled my empty well. As I sought the LORD for help, He drew me in closer to Himself and became my own personal

Bible teacher. *"I will bring him near me and he will come close to me, for who is he who will devote himself to be close to me?"* (Jeremiah 30:21) I sat at His feet many days, feasted on His Word and spent hours praying and asking to know Him more intimately. I seemed to live continually in the Book of Isaiah, a book about Israel's judgment for sin, captivity and release from captivity. In Isaiah 43:19 it describes what God was doing for me, *"See, I am doing a new thing! Now it springs up; do you not perceive it? I am making a way in the desert and streams in the wasteland."* I made the LORD my hiding place, my protector and He surrounded me with songs of deliverance. (Psalm 32:7) The LORD had stilled the storms inside to a whisper, calmed the raging sea and was guiding me to my desired haven of security.

"He stilled the storm to a whisper; the waves of the sea were hushed. They were glad when it grew calm, and he guided them to their desired haven. Let them give thanks to the LORD for his unfailing love and his wonderful deeds for men."
Psalm 107:29-31

Chapter 9

Roses in the Wilderness

"Therefore I am now going to allure her; I will lead her into the desert and speak tenderly to her. There I will give her back her vineyards, and will make the Valley of Achor (trouble) a door of hope. There she will sing as in the days of her youth, as in the day she came up out of Egypt."
Hosea 2:14-15

Whenever we hear the word **wilderness**, we usually think of a barren wasteland or a desert land where life struggles to survive. *It is not a place where we would want to go for a vacation or to live for any extended length of time!* Nothing beautiful grows there, no lush green fields, shady trees or meadows strewn with wild flowers. All you will find is prickly cactus, endless miles of shifting sand and scorching heat from the burning sun.

After the LORD led the Israelites out of the bondage of slavery in Egypt that is **exactly** where He led them—**into the wilderness**. God knew they were not ready to fight the battles that were ahead so He led them into the wilderness, the Desert of Sin, to test them and shape their character before they went into the "Promised Land". He fed them daily with manna from Heaven and provided **everything** they needed physically and *yet they still doubted Him.* (Exodus 16-17) Because of their unbelief in God's ability to deliver the enemies of the Promised Land into their hands that generation was not allowed to enter the Promised Land. They were sentenced to wander in the wilderness for forty years until their whole generation perished and then their children entered the Promised Land. God had proven faithful to them over and over and yet still they doubted Him. I have always been intrigued with their story and wondered how in the world they could have doubted God after all the miracles He performed for them. *God was about to show me just how they felt in the wilderness!* Let me tell you—I am learning to be **very careful** about how I judge the faithlessness of the people in the Bible—**lest I be next!**

In 2004, God led me into just such a wilderness experience to test me and shape my character. During this trip in the desert the Lord has dug up the unsightly weeds of my past and now fragrant roses are blooming in their place. *He started a process of sifting me like sands through an hourglass in order to purify me and make me stronger spiritually.* As the old saying goes, **"no pain, no gain"**! Although it has been a **very painful process**, I can honestly say to you now that I am **so grateful** for my trip to the wilderness. Somewhere in there, I think it has also been a trip to *"the woodshed"* for all my disobedient wanderings! It has taught me so much about the faithfulness and love of my Heavenly Father that I would never have learned any other way. Would I recommend a wilderness experience to any one else? **Absolutely!** I would even suggest you **sign up for the trip** if you have never experienced one because of the lasting effect it can have on your relationship with God. If you truly want to know God in a way that will change your life *forever*, then saddle your camel and prepare for the trip of your life. You don't need to pack anything for the trip except your Bible; God will provide **everything else** you will need! Make sure you take a notebook with you on your trip too, so you can start a journal and record the **amazing work** that God is going to do!

I started keeping a written journal one month after I arrived in the wilderness and I have now filled over five spiral notebooks. Whenever I go back to my first journal and read the things written in it I am **amazed** to see the changes **God has made** in me. A journal is also a wonderful tool of encouragement to keep track of all the promises fulfilled by God. I also wrote dates beside specific verses in my Bible wherever I felt that God was speaking a promise to me. I promise you will learn the most valuable lesson in life in your wilderness trip: *"When God is all you have, then you will know God is all you need!"* That is precisely what I have learned in my wilderness journey. **My God is enough!** God whispered to my heart one day as I sat at my easel painting, *"until you learn to be satisfied with nothing, you will never be satisfied with anything"*.

Listen to the words from Deuteronomy 32:10-13 that so perfectly describes my wilderness journey from the day I saw the eagle circling above my car.

"In a desert land he found him, in a barren and howling waste. He shielded him and cared for him; he guarded him as the apple of his eye, like an eagle that stirs up its nest and hovers over its young, that spreads its wings to catch them and carries them on its pinions. The LORD alone led him; no foreign god was with him. He made him ride on the heights of

the land and fed him with the fruit of the fields. He nourished him with honey from the rock and with oil from the flinty crag."

Manna Every Morning

    This morning as I sit at my dining room table writing this chapter I am reminded of the tender love of my Heavenly Father and how patiently He has fed and cared for me daily during my wilderness experience. As I glanced up to look at the assortment of beautiful birds that were feeding out of my feeder hanging under the tree, I noticed a beautiful red cardinal (male bird) hopping around on my patio floor. Following close behind him was a baby cardinal fluttering his wings with his mouth wide-open and waiting for his father to place a fallen seed in his mouth for nourishment. Usually the mother is the caregiver in the family; she is the one that takes care of feeding the children. However, this loving father was diligently looking for seeds to feed his offspring and then ever so tenderly placing them in the baby's mouth. The similarity to the circumstances in my own life reminded me that God was there watching over me when my mother and father were not there for me. *"Though my father and mother forsake me, the LORD will receive me."* (Psalm 27:10) My Heavenly Father is so gentle and tender in His love toward me and He has been gently feeding me these last three years. My love and trust in Him has grown tremendously over these past three years because of His tender care. I have finally come to believe in His great love for me through the difficult trials I have gone through in this wilderness experience.

    As I look back over the past three years at my financial situation I have to shake my head in utter amazement! I did receive unemployment but only for about five months since I had not worked at my last job for very long. I truly do not see how it is humanly possible to live on what I have lived on for the past three years without being in need. The LORD has taken what I had and multiplied it ten times over like He did with the five small barley loaves and two small fish. (John 6:5-13). He has used other people many times to help me financially (without my asking) when there was no art work to do in order to humble and test me. In the past, I have always run back to an office job when the work ran out but this time the LORD needed to teach me He would provide and He told me clearly, *"Now then, stand still and see this great thing the LORD is about to do before your eyes!"* (1 Samuel 12:16) I obeyed Him this time and have been blessed by His provision.

Around the first of December, 2005 the LORD spoke very clearly to me in my spirit one night as I was praying that I was getting ready to go through a really hard test but that He needed me to learn this particular lesson. He did not tell me what kind of lesson but it soon would become clear. I would not have any art work come in for eight long months but He was faithful to provide for me in so many different ways.

One incident in particular that I want to share with you happened one Wednesday morning about a week before Christmas. The apartment I live in has a mail slot on the front door where the mailman can drop my mail inside onto the floor in front of my stairs. I came downstairs past my front door that morning and went into the kitchen to fix my coffee. I sat down on my couch to have my quiet time with the LORD. I started talking to the LORD and told Him that my light bill was due the next week and I also needed to buy some groceries so I could fix Christmas dinner in case my daughter came by to eat with me. I remember reminding Him of His Word and that according to Philippians 4:19 He would meet all my needs according to His glorious riches in Christ Jesus. I told Him both of these were needs and not just wants and so I was going to buy my groceries today with the money in the bank and trust that He would provide the money I needed for my light bill due next week. I thanked him that He heard me and had already provided what I needed.

After drinking my coffee I got up to go upstairs and take a shower and get ready to go to the grocery store and as I walked by my front door I noticed an envelope sticking out of the mail slot. I thought to myself, *"Now that was not there in the door when I came downstairs, where did that come from?"* I knew the mailman had not come by yet. It was a plain white business envelope with my name typed on the front in Christmas green. I opened the envelope and there was a folded sheet of paper with a crisp one hundred dollar bill inside. There was a message typed in red and green on the paper that said, "Merry Christmas, HO, HO, HO"! I slumped down on my chair hassock in shock and then I heard that ever so sweet familiar voice of my Heavenly Father whisper, *"Go by you some groceries baby"*. I fell to my knees weeping with a heart full of thanksgiving. He had already provided my need before I even prayed. The LORD owns the cattle on a thousand hills (Psalm 50:10) and He sent me what I needed. By the way, my groceries were $99.96; He sent exactly the amount I needed with four pennies left over!

I knew the one hundred dollars had come from the LORD because no one I knew had that much extra money to put in my door and besides they would not have done it anonymously. I could not help being curious and wondering how the money was put in my door. Over the next couple of days I wondered could the LORD have possibly sent an angel to put the money in my door. On Friday afternoon I turned on my radio to listen to some Christmas music as I had just finished asking the

LORD, *"was it an angel"*. All of a sudden the words to the song playing said there are angels that walk among us in the times of our darkest needs and I knew he was telling me **an angel's hands had placed the money in my door!** *"Praise the LORD, you his angels, you mighty ones who do his bidding, who obey his word. Praise the LORD, all his heavenly hosts, you his servants who do his bidding, who obey his word."* (Psalm 103:20-21)

Whenever I share with others, what the LORD has been doing in my life over the past few years I often joke with them and say, *"I go out my back door and gather my **manna every morning**"*. I guess there really is more truth in there than jest! That morning the LORD put my manna in the front door and I did not even have to go out and gather it! Well, I guess that is not exactly true, I did have to go to the grocery store and bring it home! *"Then the LORD said to Moses, "I will rain down bread from heaven for you. The people are to go out each day and gather enough for that day. In this way I will test them and see whether they will follow my instructions."* (Exodus 16:4)

No More Fear

If you were to ask me what chain of bondage was one of the most important ones that the LORD has broken in my life, I guess I would have to say **"No More Fear"**. Fear has ruled over me most of my life and governed most of the decisions I made. I had learned you could not trust anyone and I was afraid to **completely trust God either**! I was afraid that God would let me down just like all of the other people in my life. That has turned out to be the most important lesson He wanted to teach me. Hear this promise given to me in the beginning of the LORD'S work of breaking the chains of fear. *"The cowering* *prisoners will soon be set free; they will not die in their dungeon, nor will they lack bread."* (Isaiah 51:14) I had run so many times from this lesson but this time my Heavenly Father blocked my every path and built a hedge around me to keep me still. Listen to His words to me, *"Therefore I will block her path with thorn bushes; I will wall her in so that she cannot find her way."* (Hosea 2:6) Over the past three years I have pulled **quite a few** of those thorns out of my backside from trying to find a way out of this hedge my Heavenly Father has built so tightly around me. In the beginning, I kicked and screamed for a while like a horse that is being broken for riding but the Father has patiently waited for me to calm down and stop bucking Him! *I have learned to sing now when I see the saddle coming!* He knows just what we need and how long we need it! Trust me, there is no point in trying to sweet talk Him into letting you out before your time because the more you whine, the longer you will have to stay! This is one of the hardest lessons and it has taken me a good while to learn it—the LORD hates murmuring and complaining. Listen to what Numbers 11:1 says about how much God hates complaining, *"Now the people complained about their hardships in the hearing of the LORD, and when he heard them his anger was aroused. Then fire from the LORD burned among them and consumed some of the outskirts of the camp."* **Oh, how I love Moses and those Israelites in the wilderness, I have learned so many things from their mistakes!**

When we walk in fear then we cannot be walking in faith! If fear walks in the front door then faith goes out the back and we cannot please God without faith. I had the order backwards from what God desired. I had let fear push faith out the back door and so He had to change my order of things. Hebrews 11:6 tells us so clearly, *"and without faith it is impossible to please*

God, because anyone who comes to him must believe that he exists and that he rewards those who earnestly seek him." I did not want to be afraid that God would let me down but because I did not know Him intimately I could not trust Him. Through the constant reading of God's Word and prayer I was getting to know the LORD intimately and learning to trust Him and my faith in Him was growing.

I have had to cling tightly to the LORD through my wilderness trials for **everything** and I have learned to trust **only Him completely**. He knocked all of my crutches out from under me so that I would have only His weight to lean on. My growing faith in my Heavenly Father has pushed all of my fear out the back door and God has closed the door of fear in my life. Whatever door God closes no one can open again! (Revelation 3:7) Satan tries to sneak fear back in through a window every now and again but I just remind him that God is my Father and He lives inside me and He is greater than Satan. 1 John 4:4 says, *You, dear children, are from God and have overcome them, because the one who is in you is greater than the one who is in the world."*

The Lord has also taught me through Peter's example *to keep my eyes on Jesus and not on my circumstances*. I am so much like Peter, always speaking out and **putting my foot in my mouth**! Whenever I started looking around at what I was doing, trying to make a living painting full time with no benefits and very little salary, I started to sink! Panic would wash over me like the waves in the water did with Peter when he looked around and took his eyes off Jesus and I would start to come unglued.

Many times I cried out to the LORD that I wanted to go back to an office job where I had the security of a weekly paycheck coming in and benefits. Then the LORD would take me by the hand and remind me how **unreliable** that situation **had just proven** in my life and that I needed to keep my eyes on Him and trust **Him only** for my security. He showed me from Psalm 103:2-5 that He provided all the benefits I needed. *"Praise the LORD, O my soul, and forget not all his benefits—who forgives all your sins and heals all your diseases, who redeems your life from the pit and crowns you with love and compassion, who satisfies your desires with good things, so that your youth is renewed like the eagle's."* He wanted me to step out of my boat of security in an office and walk **on the water with Him**. If I would just keep looking at Jesus—I too could do the impossible and walk on the water. *"'Come,' he said. Then Peter got down out of the boat, walked on the water and came toward Jesus. But when he saw the wind he was afraid and, beginning to sink, cried out, 'Lord, save me!' Immediately Jesus reached out his hand and caught him. 'You of little faith,' he said, 'why did you doubt?'"* (Matthew 14:29-31) WOW, it has been so much fun to walk on the water with Jesus! He has not let me sink—not even once!

The LORD has led me to so many precious scripture passages about not fearing anything and used them to help me overcome my fears. I read them over and over daily until they sank into my spirit. I have learned how vitally important it is to speak out loud the promises of God into the physical realm. When we speak God's promises from His Word aloud it is the same as God speaking them. God has taught me how important it is to speak positive things out of my mouth instead of all the negative things I used to say because the tongue holds the power of life or death. *"Death and life **are** in the power of the tongue, and they that love it shall eat the fruit thereof."* (Proverbs 18:21) I wrote encouraging verses out on paper and taped them all over my house, especially on the mirror in my bathroom. I read them first thing in the morning at the beginning of my day and every night before I went to bed.

Did you know there are over three hundred verses in the Bible about not being in fear? That is enough verses to read a different verse about fear every day of the year. One of my favorite verses that sustained me during so many days filled with fear comes from Isaiah. Not only did it tell me **not to fear** it also said that God had chosen me and HE **had not rejected me.** Oh, how I embraced this verse as my very own because I had been rejected by so many people my entire life! *"I said, 'You are my servant'; I have chosen you and have not rejected you. So do not fear for I am with you; do not be dismayed, for I am your God. I will strengthen you and help you; I will uphold you with my righteous right hand."* (Isaiah 41:9-10) It comforted me so many times when I felt fearful, discouraged and alone. *How could I be afraid when Almighty God was holding my hand?*

So often during these past months the LORD has spoken to me through nature and then given me scriptures that said almost the exact thing I had seen. It has truly been amazing! He also used a dream early one morning to paint a vivid picture for me that I was not to be afraid. Just before I awakened I saw a hand coming down out of the clouds in the sky reaching out toward me. As it came closer I noticed a nail scar in the palm of the hand. I knew that it must be Jesus' hand but when I woke up I thought how strange it was that there was **only one hand** in the dream. I lay there quietly, thought about the dream for a while and tried to figure out what it meant. I finally realized it was the LORD'S left hand extended as if to take me by my right hand to hold hands with me. He was telling me through the dream that He was holding my hand and I was not to be afraid. The next day He led me to this scripture from Isaiah that confirmed what I thought He was telling me through the dream. *"For I am the LORD, your God, who takes hold of your right hand and says to you, Do not fear; I will help you. Do not be afraid, O worm Jacob, O little Israel, for I myself will help you, declares the LORD, your Redeemer, the Holy One of Israel."* (Isaiah 41:13-14)

On another occasion during the eight months without any artwork, I was experiencing a lot of fear about my financial situation. One morning I was sitting on my couch and reading my Bible for comfort and strength. I looked out of my window and began to stare at my bird bath beside the window. All of a sudden tiny sparrows started landing on the bird bath until finally I counted six sparrows in the water at the same time! This was an unusual sight because usually there is only a couple in there together at one time. They started splashing and playing in the water together without a care in the world. I immediately remembered the verses where Jesus talked about the sparrows and how their Heavenly Father watches over them. I turned in my Bible to Matthew 10 and started reading verses 29 through 31. *"Are not two sparrows sold for a penny? Yet not one of them will fall to the ground apart from the will of your Father. And even the very hairs of your head are all numbered. So don't be afraid; you are worth more than many sparrows."* All of a sudden the last one, verse 31, leaped off the page at me as if it were a blinking neon sign. This is how God often speaks to us when He has a particular truth that He wants to convey to us. Listen again to Matthew 10:31, *"So don't be afraid; you are worth more than many sparrows."* There I was watching a bird bath full of **many sparrows** that the LORD had sent to me to tell me **not to be afraid** that He knew everything about my situation and He wanted me to live as carefree as these little birds.

There are too many other numerous instances, where my Father has spoken clearly through nature to calm my fears and reassure me of His abiding presence, to tell you all of them. Every one of them He has poured into my heart like a soothing ointment to calm the fear and anxiety within. With every one of the occurrences He has given me scripture to confirm what He was showing me. I have now finally come to a place where the things that used to rattle me do not frighten me anymore. I am not afraid anymore that God won't come through and I will not be able to pay my bills or buy my groceries. I am not afraid the He is not going to meet my needs! Sometimes He waits to the last minute but He has never failed to show up on time! He is **never late** and He is **rarely early** either but that is where our trust has a chance to grow.

As part of my financial lessons in overcoming fear I have also learned to tithe the first ten percent of any money I receive from the LORD and watch Him make the remaining 90% go farther than reasonably possible! During the last three years He enrolled me in a course called "Finances a Little at the Time" in order to teach me to manage my money! Unfortunately, He has not allowed me to graduate from this course yet! When you do not have much money to work with you learn to be very careful how you spend what little you do have! *It is a great way to learn but a tough way to live!* It has been a painful course to work through but I am learning some **well-needed** and **overdue** lessons that I never learned from a parent growing up! God has remained faithful however to his promise in Malachi 3:10 to pour out blessings and provide a way where it seemed impossible. *"I am making a way in the desert and streams in the wasteland."* (Isaiah 43:19)

I can actually say with confidence now that I know whatever comes into my life has passed through His loving hands and so I will not fear. *"The LORD is with me; I will not be afraid. What *can man do to me?"* (Psalm 118:6) I would never have said that before because I did not believe it deep down in my heart three years ago. I did not understand the tender love of my Heavenly Father because everything I had known about love was painful. My whole life, the only love I ever knew **hurt me** out of anger and so I was afraid of God's love for me too. The Father has shown me that **in His love there is no fear because His love is perfect!** 1 John 4:16 & 18 tells us that God is love and that perfect love casts out fear. My Heavenly Father's relentless pursuit of me has given me the knowledge of God's perfect love and has truly conquered the dreaded fear in my life. Because I trust in Him, I will not be shaken. *"Those who trust in the LORD are like Mount Zion, which cannot be shaken but endures forever."* (Psalm 125:1)

Somewhere Above the Rainbow

What does a **promise** mean? Well, according to Webster, in its noun form a "promise" means one's pledge to another that one will or will not do something; ground for hope; and indication of future excellence. In its verb form a "promise" means to engage to do or give; give one's word to; afford hope or expectation (of).[5] A promise can be sealed by making a covenant or solemn agreement. The God of the Bible is a covenant making God. In the Bible a covenant may be made between nations, between individuals and friends or between a husband and wife. Throughout God's Word He makes covenants with those who love Him and follow Him and He always faithfully keeps His covenant promises. Usually the covenant contracts were accompanied by signs, sacrifices, and a solemn oath which sealed the relationship with promises of blessings for obedience and curses for disobedience.

The most **important covenant of God** made to mankind was through **the blood of His son Jesus**. One of the first covenant promises to appear in the Bible in the Old Testament was made with Noah. In Genesis after the flood had subsided and Noah, his family and all of the animals came out of the ark God made a covenant promise to Noah that never again would He destroy the world with a flood and the seasons would thereafter always come as expected. (Genesis 6-9) As a visible sign of God's covenant promise to all humankind, He set a rainbow in the clouds that would appear after the rain to remind the world that He keeps his promises. *"And God said, 'This is the sign of the covenant I am making between me and you and every living creature with you, a covenant for all generations to come: I have set my rainbow in the clouds and it will be the sign of the covenant between me and the earth. Whenever I bring clouds over the earth and the rainbow appears in the clouds, I will remember my covenant between me and you and all living creatures of every kind. Never again will the waters become a flood to destroy all life. Whenever the rainbow appears in the clouds, I will see it and remember the everlasting covenant between God and all living creatures of every kind on the earth."* (Genesis 9:12-16) To this day, the rainbow still appears in the clouds as a reminder of God's faithfulness to His word.

My Heavenly Father has used the rainbow in a very personal way over the past year to remind me that He keeps His promises and He is still watching over me. **'Somewhere above the rainbow'** in the highest Heavens my Father is on His throne and He has not forgotten me! He has sent so many rainbows my way that I have to chuckle even now when I think about all of them. I am not talking about the big kind of arched rainbows that appear in the rain clouds after a storm. No, my Father has sent me numerous little small rainbows that have appeared in just a tiny patch of cloud on a sunny day and many other unusual places. They always seem to appear just when I walk to the door to look out or when I am driving in the car. On two different occasions, I have even seen a complete circular rainbow around the sun on a cloud-filled day that reminded me of the rainbow that encircles God's throne. (Revelation 4:3) All of the rainbows were there just when I needed to be cheered up and reminded that God was with me. He had not forgotten me or His promises of help and healing.

After seeing a rainbow, God would then lead me to many verses about His covenant promises. I would meditate on the verses until the promises watered my heart and produced seeds of hope within me. One of the most beautiful verses the LORD has given me to remind me of His covenant promises that has ministered so much to me during the last few years comes from the book of Zechariah. Listen to the beautiful words in Zechariah 9:11-12, *"As for you, because of the blood of my covenant with you, I will free your prisoners, from the waterless pit. Return to your fortress, O prisoners of hope; even now I announce that I will restore twice as much to you."* God was telling me that because of my blood covenant with Him through His son Jesus, He was going to free me from all of the pits that have so hopelessly trapped me and stolen away my life. By returning to Him, my fortress, He would make me a prisoner of hope instead of despair and He was going to give me back twice as much of everything that the devil has stolen from me. *He has indeed become my fortress of hope!*

We all know about personal pan size pizzas and probably have eaten them at least once in our lives but have you ever had your very own **personal size rainbow**? Well, once again God has outdone Himself in my life with His sense of humor! Try to visualize with me how amazing this scenario was as I describe it to you. It was Friday, May 11, 2007 and I had gone for a walk earlier in the morning as I often do to spend time in worship and praise to the LORD. As I walked along I prayed and asked the LORD to reveal His great love for me because I was feeling very lonely and I needed to feel His love for me. In John 14:21 it says, *"He who loves me will be loved by my Father, and I too will love him and show myself to him."* He was about to show me His love again!

Then around 1:00 p.m. that day, I decided to sit out on my patio and read a book a friend had recommended about a man's trip to Heaven. I should have been painting but I wasn't in the mood to paint and so I decided to finish reading my book instead. I needed to get some sunshine and fresh air anyway so since a few trees shaded my patio it was the perfect place to sit and read. It was a beautiful sunny day, mixed with only a few intermittent clouds. I have a small water fountain on my patio and it would be very peaceful sitting there listening to the trickling water. I had been outside reading about an hour when all of a sudden a tiny arched full color spectrum rainbow about two inches long appeared on the left hand side of my book. *Well, I blinked my eyes thinking I was imagining the rainbow!* No it was not my imagination, when I opened my eyes back up the rainbow was still there. I blinked again, still there! I started moving the book around thinking something was causing the reflection to appear on the book but everywhere I moved the book—**the rainbow stayed right there on the page**. I started looking around to see if I could, figure out what was causing this phenomenon but there was nothing around to create the reflection of a rainbow. *Nothing that is in this world!* God had sent me my own **personal rainbow** right there on the book I was reading about **Heaven**! The rainbow must have stayed on the page for several minutes and by this time, I started laughing hilariously aloud. I imagined the Father and Jesus sitting in Heaven laughing and saying, *"She is going to love this special effect"*! After I stopped laughing and thanked the Father for His special gift, I immediately remembered my verse from Zechariah. This time, up close and personal, the LORD once again reminded me that *He would never break His covenant promises to me, He loved me and He remembered me.*

Each time that I think about my **"personal pan rainbow"**, it brings a big smile to my face to think that the Ancient of Days, Almighty God loves me so much He would take time out from running the world to send me a kiss in the shape of a rainbow. God sent me a sign to seal our relationship and promise me blessings because of my obedience to Him. Just this morning in my quiet time my Father once again reminded me that He is fulfilling His covenant promises to me through a verse in Leviticus. Chapter 26 tells about the rewards for obedience and punishment for disobedience to the LORD. Leviticus 26:9 says, *"I will look on you with favor and make you fruitful and increase your numbers, and I will keep my covenant with you."* As I continued to read, I found the promise God has been fulfilling in my life in verse 13. *"I am the LORD your God, who brought you out of Egypt so that you would no longer be slaves to the Egyptians; I broke the bars of your yoke and enabled you to walk with heads held high."* In the Old Testament, Egypt usually represents the world or sin. God truly has rescued me out of the world of sin, broken the yokes from my back and enabled me to walk with my head held high for the first time in my life. ***Wow, now that is something to sing over the rainbow about!***

Why, you might be asking, does God choose to speak to me visually so often the way He does? I have asked myself that exact same question so many times and there are several answers that I have come up with. First, I think since I have been such a **hardheaded, slow learner** that God decided He needed to use visual aids to get my attention! *I have to admit I do learn better with visuals!* Second, I think He does it because my being an artist makes me a very visual person and I love special effects! I appreciate all of the beauty around me that God has created and I am forever attentive to the smallest details in creation. *Creation itself is the greatest work of art ever painted by the "Master Artist" of the Universe.* God very lovingly tucked away that part of Himself in me when He chose to bestow the talent of art upon me. I always look for Him in nature everywhere I go! Thirdly, and probably the most important reason He sends me visuals is because I was so hungry to know Him and His presence with me! I have cried out in prayer and sought to know Him with all my heart and I have found Him—up close and personal! *"Then you will call upon me and come and pray to me, and I will listen to you. You will seek me and find me when you seek me with all your heart."* (Jeremiah 29:12-13)

He Is My Husband

Miracle of all miracles the LORD has performed in my life is that I can now say with all honesty and sincerity that *the only man I need in my life to make me happy is Jesus*. Three years ago, I would never have believed that I could finally say, *"I don't need a man anymore to make me happy!"* I think most of my friends still **gasp in shock** every time that statement comes out of my mouth! Even in the beginning days of this journey in 2004, I still was searching for a man to share my life with. I still felt so alone that I tried the internet match sites once again for a couple of months. However, the LORD blocked all the paths with anyone I tried to date because He wanted to teach me **He was all I needed**. *"She will chase after her lovers but not catch them; she will look for them but not find them. Then she will say, 'I will go back to my husband as at first, for then I was better off than now.'"* (Hosea 2:7)

It is really kind of funny now as I think back on the different ways the LORD has removed people from my life in order to protect me and keep me solely to Him. The more intimate time I spent alone with the LORD, the more I realized that **His** was the **real love** I had been seeking so desperately. The more my Father revealed Himself and His character to me *the more in love with Him I fell*. I have loved every intimate moment we have spent together. I have now finally found someone that wants to spend every waking moment with me and never tires of my neediness for His attention and love. He thinks I am beautiful, flawless, and I am precious and honored in His sight. *"Since you are precious and honored in my sight, and because I love you."* (Isaiah 43:4) *"All beautiful you are, my darling; there is no flaw in you."* (Song of Songs 4:7)

One night as I sat in the tub soaking my aching muscles I started crying and talking to the LORD. I told Him how lonely I was and that I wanted a husband. Through the still soft voice inside the LORD asked me, *"what is it a husband does?"* I thought that was a curious question but then I told Him that a husband provides love, friendship, financial security, a home, food, and emotional support. I will never forget His reply to me spoken in almost a sad sort of voice, *"have I not provided those very things for you and better than any of your other husbands?"* Then the LORD said to me, *"I am your husband and I will take care of you."* Hear His words from Isaiah 54:5, *"For your Maker is your husband—the LORD Almighty is his name—the Holy One of Israel is your Redeemer; he is called the God of all the earth."* Even though I have spent a great deal of time by myself over the past three years, I have never felt alone because of the LORD'S very real presence with me. I know He is with me and I am never alone. He has sustained me and comforted me. He has put a new song in my heart and taught me to sing even in the midst of my trials. *"My servants will sing out of the joy of their hearts."* (Isaiah 65:14) Jeremiah 31:13 tells what the LORD has done in my life, *"I will turn their mourning into gladness; I will give them comfort and joy instead of sorrow."* The LORD has given me a crown of beauty instead of the ashes of my past, the oil of gladness for all my sadness and new garments of praise instead of the heavy spirit of despair I wore my whole life. (Isaiah 61:3)

I have **finally** found the husband who will **never leave me or be unfaithful.** *"I will betroth you in faithfulness, and you will acknowledge the LORD."* (Hosea 4:20) As a believer in Christ I am called His bride, He is my bridegroom, and He is rejoicing over me. *"As a young man marries a maiden, so will your sons marry you; as a bridegroom rejoices over his bride, so will your God rejoice over you."* (Isaiah 62:5) He has betrothed me to Himself forever and I will never be alone again. *"I will betroth you to myself forever; I will betroth you in righteousness and justice, in love and compassion."* (Hosea 4:19) He **will never reject me** and **leave me for someone else.** *"Never will I leave you; never will I forsake you."* (Hebrews 13:5) When I sit in His presence I am filled with a joy and peace that words can never describe. *"In thy presence is fullness of joy; at thy right hand there are pleasures forever more."* (Psalm 16:11 KJV) At last I have found the 'Prince' to whom I can say, *"My beloved is mine, and I am his."* (Song of Songs 2:16)

At the time of my writing this book, I am still traveling in the wilderness but I am no longer concerned with when the trip will end! I have learned to enjoy the desert view, smell the cactus roses (not too closely) and sing a song of joy along the way until I arrive at my next destination. My Father knows what things in me still need to be purged by the burning hot sands and when **He thinks** I am ready; He will open the hedge and lead the way. *"The LORD will guide you always, he will satisfy your needs in a sun-scorched land and will strengthen your frame. You will be like a well-watered garden, like a spring whose waters never fail."* (Isaiah 58:11) My Father led me into the wilderness and His cultivation work in me has produced **roses in the wilderness!**

"The LORD will surely comfort Zion and will look with compassion on all her ruins; he will make her deserts like Eden, her wastelands like the garden of the LORD. Joy and gladness will be found in her, thanksgiving and the sound of singing."
Isaiah 51:3

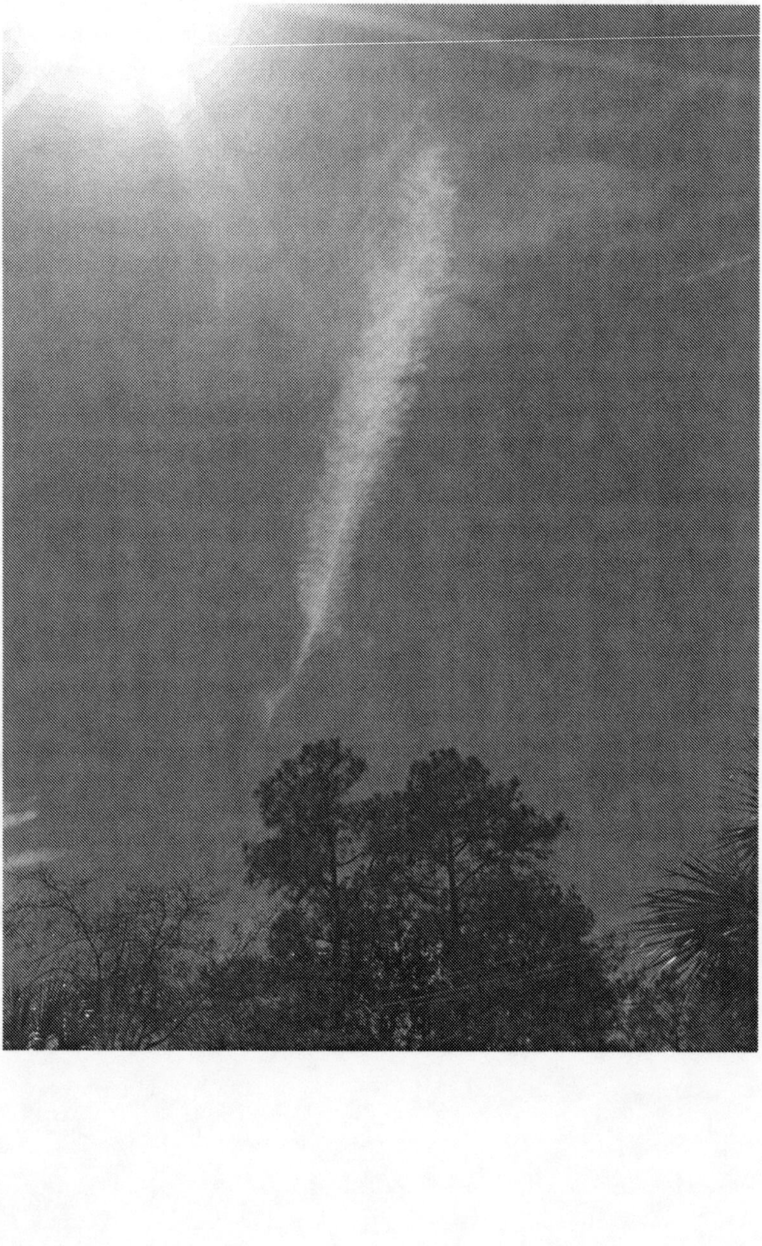

Chapter 10

Love Notes from My Father

"The LORD appeared to us in the past, saying: 'I have loved you with an everlasting love; I have drawn you with loving kindness'."
Jeremiah 31:3

If you were to ask me what verse in the Bible is my favorite that most accurately describes my entire life's journey with the LORD I would have to tell you it is Jeremiah 31:3, the verse quoted above. I would also have to admit that this verse has become a more vivid reality in my life since 2004. My Heavenly Father has led me to meditate on this particular verse many times in my quiet times with Him. I even wrote the words "a never-ending or changing love" in the margin of my Bible beside this verse to remind myself **how great His love is**. I continually quoted it to myself aloud and it was one of the verses I had taped on my bathroom mirror. On February 24, 2006 the Father was going to show me **just how much** He loves me through His greatest 'visual effect' thus far!

During my beginning stay at home, I tried to go for a walk a couple of times a week to get some exercise and build up my strength. I usually wore my headphones and listened to praise music while I walked. It was always a wonderful time of worship and fellowship with my Father. We had experienced a few unusually warm days for February and some of the spring flowers had already begun to unfold their petals from their long winter's nap. The pink Japanese magnolia trees were already in full bloom and they were breathtaking. I remember clearly the LORD through His Holy Spirit telling me, *"Let's go for a walk today and take your camera with you so you can take some pictures of the beautiful flowers for painting."* It seemed like a good idea to me so I grabbed my camera, put my headphones on and out the door I went. I walked a few hundred yards and then I stopped, looked up into the clear blue sky to pray to my Father. I will never forget what I said, *"Oh Abba, write me love notes as we walk along so that I will know how much you love me, I've just got to know how much you love me."* My thoughts about how He would show me were that He might send some butterflies my way or just wash waves of love over me through a real sense of His presence with me. Never in my wildest dreams did I expect what the LORD was about to send me!

When I finished praying, I walked out of the driveway of my apartments, turned to the right and walked down the main road I live on. I had walked about two hundred yards and decided to turn into a nearby subdivision to photograph a palm tree that was in someone's yard. As I turned around and raised my camera to take the picture, there in the sky was a HUGE cloud in the shape of a **perfectly formed feather quill**, complete with little white lines underneath. Instantly I heard my Abba Father whisper in my spirit, *"There baby, I'm writing you love notes!"* Well, I can tell you I felt like Moses at the burning bush! I wanted to fall down on my knees and then my face in worship but I was afraid someone would call 911! After I gathered my wits about me, I started snapping pictures of this awesome wonder that God had painted in the sky to show His **never-ending, everlasting love for me.** I immediately began to praise Him with a sense of awe and humility for the love note He wrote to me in the sky with His own hand. It says in Nahum 1:3 that *"the clouds are the dust of his feet"* but I can tell you with all sincerity that *I felt like the dust at His feet that day*! That old saying *"you could have knocked me over with a feather"* was most appropriate for the occasion! The feather quill stayed there in the sky for at least five minutes or more, never changing or moving as I gazed up in stupefied wonder worshipping at His feet! *I was dumbstruck to say the least!*

I am sure the Father and Jesus were probably laughing hilariously at the look on my face when I first saw the feather quill. *It must have been priceless!* I hope there will be visual videos in Heaven so I can replay that moment again just to see the look on my face myself. The Father TRULY outdid Himself in my life that day! If there are better 'visual effects' than this still to come, I do not know if my heart will be able to stand them! That one was an Oscar Award winner! *"He makes the clouds his chariot and rides on the wings of the wind."* (Psalm 104:3)

Not only had the LORD again painted an amazing picture in the sky for me but also this time **He made sure** I had my camera with me to **capture the moment**! Needless to say I have printed numerous copies of the picture, one of which is in this book, and I put one in every room of my apartment. It even crossed my mind to wallpaper my bedroom with the pictures but I did not think my landlord would appreciate the effect! It has been an amazing encouraging reminder of God's awesome wonder working love for me. I have showed the picture to a lot of people and some of them have even asked me how I made the picture. I just smile and tell them **God did it—I didn't!** Every time I look at it, I hear His sweet words again *"there baby, I'm writing you love notes"* and my heart leaps with warm joy. I still find it hard to believe that the great God of this vast universe heard my earnest prayer for reassurance of His love for me and in less than three minutes, He answered me in a way I could never have imagined. *"Now to him who is able to do exceedingly abundantly above all that we ask or think, according to the power that worketh in us."* (Ephesians 3:20) The Father definitely did **exceedingly** and **abundantly** more than I could **ever have imagined!**

After all God has done over the past three years to show me His love, I finally believe my Heavenly Father loves me. He has also again used the *pillars of cloud* on two occasions during my stay here in the wilderness. On these two different occasions He put the *two pillar clouds*, one on each side of the sun, as a reminder that He is guiding me and that I am going in the right direction. He has surely drawn me with loving kindness. Whenever Satan comes around whispering his lies that my Father has forgotten me and does not love me, I just point to the picture of the feather quill and say to him, *"really, then why did My Father write me a love note in the sky?"* My Heavenly Father wanted me to know how much He loves me and I believe He wants to do the same thing for you if you earnestly seek after Him to know Him.

The cross of Calvary is the ultimate sign of His love for us because He gave up his beloved Son Jesus to prove His love for us. (John 3:16) The Bible is our love letter from the Father telling us **how much He loves us**. The abuse and insecurity in my life though had made it hard for me to understand and believe there truly was such unconditional love. I desperately needed someone to notice and love me and so God chose to show me in many extraordinary ways that **He** loved and noticed me. I cried out to know I was loved and My Heavenly Father has ridden through the skies with **awesome wonders** to show me His love. *"There is no one like the God of Israel, who rides on the heavens to help you and on the clouds in his majesty."* (Deuteronomy 33:26)

"He is your praise; he is your God, who performed for you those great and awesome wonders you saw with your own eyes."
Deuteronomy 10:21

Chapter 11

Happily Forever After

"I will betroth you to me forever; I will betroth you in righteousness and justice, in love and compassion. I will betroth you in faithfulness, and you will acknowledge the LORD."
Hosea 2:19-20

All of my life has been spent waiting, looking and dreaming for the day my handsome 'prince charming' would come galloping to my rescue on his beautiful white stallion. Dressed in his royal robes and riding forth in majestic power and splendor. He would sweep me up in his arms, whisper tender words of love, wipe away all my tears of pain, and take me to his far away kingdom where we would live "happily ever after". ***WAIT**, what is that I hear?* I hear the sound of thundering hooves and they are galloping closer. *Do you hear them?* Now I hear the sound of trumpets announcing a royal arrival! *Do you hear them?* **OH look**, there He comes in all His splendor and majesty! A magnificent milky white stallion is riding toward me with a conquering rider dressed in dazzling white garments with golden sash and crowns of gold upon His head. He glows like brilliant fire from a furnace. The light from His face is radiant; it sparkles like thousands of diamonds in the sunshine. *Can you see Him?* Oh my, He takes my breath away, I cannot speak! My heart is pounding with excitement, I knew some day my 'Prince' would come but even in my wildest imaginations I never expected anything like this!

As this royal 'Prince' rides closer, I fall to my knees wonder struck and speechless. I fall down on my face before His brilliant presence in fear and trembling. Beams of rainbow light surround Him encircling Him like a halo from Heaven. I can hear His powerful voice, like mighty rushing waters; call my name ever so tenderly. His words to me are like a symphony of music composed for my ears only. As He dismounts His royal steed, He walks toward me, takes my right hand in His and says, *"Do not be afraid, I am the first and the last 'Prince' and I have come to rescue you my darling and take you away to live with me forever because you have stolen my heart"*. There is a sweet smell of fragrance filling the air with each step He takes toward me. Then He begins to sing a song of love to me and tells me how beautiful I am to Him, how much He has always loved me. Suddenly, I remember my filthy rags that I am wearing and look down at them in embarrassment and shame. *But what is this, what has happened? I can hardly believe my eyes!* I turn to gaze at my reflection in the water of the well where I have come to draw water. As I lean over the water, I can see that my rags have been transformed into the most magnificent golden embroidered gown that I have ever seen. There on my head sits a crown of gold that outshines the sun and magnificent jewels adorn my neck. **Wow!** *Who is this lovely vision of a woman I see in the water, surely it cannot be me!* This 'Prince' seems to read my mind and turns me around gently toward Him and whispers with eyes full of love, *"All beautiful you are, my* *darling; there is no flaw in you. I will love you forever with a never ending love"*. Then He sweeps me up in His powerful arms and whisks me away on the wind in the twinkling of an eye. We are riding together through the clouds as one and He is taking me with Him to His Mansions on high where He has prepared a home for me. There in the distance I can see the golden streets of the Heavenly City where He will reign as **King of Kings** forever and ever with me by His side. Our marriage supper is ready, all is prepared, and the invitations have already been extended to those who will come. ***Let the joyous celebration begin!***

Am I dreaming—can this 'fairy tale' really come true? **No**, it is not a dream or a "fairy tale" but a true story of promised love and redemption. Jesus, the 'Prince of Peace', 'Lord of Lords' and 'King of Kings' wants to ride to your rescue and help you experience this same tale of love too—if you will let Him. Christ is the only 'Prince' who can ever fulfill our *happily forever after*! I would like to repeat for you, with God's own mouth, my sweet romantic love story taken from the words of the Bible, God's love letter to His children. After all, God was the creator of romance in the very beginning and He still wants more than anything to sweep you off your feet!

"Listen! My lover! Look! Here he comes, leaping across the mountains, bounding over the hills. (Song of Songs 2:8) Who is this, robed in splendor, striding forward in the greatness of his strength? (Isaiah 63:1) I saw heaven standing open and there before me was a white horse, whose rider is called Faithful and True. His eyes are like blazing fire, and on his head are many crowns. (Revelation 19:11-12) I turned around to see the voice that was speaking to me. And when I turned I saw seven golden lampstands, and among the lampstands was someone 'like a son

of man', dressed in a robe reaching down to his feet and with a golden sash around his chest. His head and hair were white like wool, as white as snow, and his eyes were like blazing fire. His feet were like bronze glowing in a furnace, and his voice was like the sound of rushing waters. (Rev. 1:12-15) His face was like the sun shining in all its brilliance. When I saw him, I fell at his feet as though dead. Then he placed his right hand on me and said: 'Do not be afraid. I am the First and the Last'. (Rev 1:16-17) I saw that from what appeared to be his waist up he looked like glowing metal, as if full of fire, and that from there down he looked like fire; and brilliant light surrounded him. Like the appearance of a rainbow in the clouds on a rainy day, so was the radiance around him. This was the appearance of the likeness of the glory of the Lord. When I saw it, I fell facedown, and I heard the voice of one speaking. (Ezekiel 1:27-28) And the one who sat there had the appearance of jasper and carnelian. A rainbow, resembling an emerald, encircled the throne. (Revelation 4:3) O LORD my God, you are very great; you are clothed with splendor and majesty. He wraps himself in light as with a garment. (Psalm 104:1-2) Who is this that appears like the dawn, fair as the moon, bright as the sun, majestic as the stars in procession? (Song of Songs 6:10) All thy garments smell of myrrh, and aloes, and cassia, out of the ivory palaces, whereby they have made thee glad. (Psalm 45:8 KJV) Pleasing is the fragrance of your perfumes; your name is like perfume poured out. No wonder maidens love you! (Song of Songs 1:3) My lover is radiant and ruddy, outstanding among ten thousand. His head is purest gold; his hair is wavy and black as a raven. His eyes are like doves by the water streams, washed in milk, mounted like jewels. His cheeks are like beds of spice yielding perfume. His lips are like lilies dripping with myrrh. His arms are rods of gold set with chrysolite. His body is like polished ivory decorated with sapphires. His legs are pillars of marble set on bases of pure gold. His appearance is like Lebanon, choice as its cedars. His mouth is sweetness itself; he is altogether lovely." (Song of Songs 5:10-16) Because of His great power and mighty strength. (Isaiah 40:26)

"The LORD, the King of Israel, is with you; never again will you fear any harm. (Zephaniah 3:15) For I am the LORD, your God, who takes hold of your right hand and says to you, Do not fear; I will help you. (Isaiah 41:13) The LORD your God is with you, he is mighty to save. He will take great delight in you, he will quiet you with his love, he will rejoice over you with singing. (Zephaniah 3:17) I have loved you with an everlasting love; (Jeremiah 31:3) How beautiful you are, my darling! Oh, how beautiful! (Song of Songs 4:1) All beautiful you are, my darling; there is no flaw in you. (Song of Songs 4:7) Your lips are like a scarlet ribbon; your mouth is lovely. (Song of Songs 4:3) You have stolen my heart, my sister, my bride; you have stolen my heart with one glance of your eyes, with one jewel of your necklace. How delightful is your love, my sister, my bride! How much more pleasing is your love than wine, and the fragrance of your perfume than any spice! (Song of Songs 4:9-10) Those who look to him are radiant; their faces are never covered with shame. (Psalm 34:5) The angel said to those who were standing before him, 'Take off his filthy clothes.' Then he said to Joshua, 'See, I have taken away your sin, and I will put rich garments on you.' (Zechariah 3:4) All glorious is the princess within her chamber; her gown is interwoven with gold. In embroidered garments she is led to the king; her virgin companions follow her and are brought to you. They are led in with joy and gladness; they enter the palace of the king." (Psalm 45:13-15)

"For the LORD himself will come down from heaven, with a loud command, with the voice of the archangel and with the trumpet call of God, and the dead in Christ will rise first. (1 Thessalonians 4:16) Listen, I tell you a mystery: We will not all sleep, but we will all be changed—in a flash, in the twinkling of an eye, at the last trumpet. For the trumpet will sound, the dead will be raised imperishable, and we will be changed. For the perishable must clothe itself with the imperishable, and the mortal with immortality. (1 Corinthians 15:51-53) He makes the clouds his chariot and rides on the wings of the wind. (Psalm 104:3) In my Father's house are many mansions; if it were not so, I would have told you. I go to prepare a place for you. And if I go to prepare a place for you, I will come again, and receive you unto myself, that where I am, there ye may be also. (John 14:2-3 KJV) The great street of the city was of pure gold, like transparent glass. (Revelation 21:21) He has taken me to the banquet hall, and his banner over me is love. (Song of Songs 2:4) Let us rejoice and be glad and give him glory! For the wedding of the Lamb has come, and his bride has made herself ready. (Revelation 19:7) Then the angel said to me; 'Write: Blessed are those who are invited to the wedding supper of the Lamb!' And he added, 'These are the true words of God.' (Revelation 19:9) And they will reign for ever and ever." (Revelation 22:5)

Jesus now stands before you in all **His magnificent splendor,** extending His nail scarred hand to you and waiting for your romance to begin. Are you ready to let Him sweep you off your feet, to fall head over heels in love with Him? ***That is the desire of His heart you know—how about yours?*** All you have to do is pray and tell Him that you want to fall hopelessly in love with Him forever. After you pray, sit back and watch the romance begin! In 2004, I cried out to Him and told Him, *"I have got to know how much you love me or I cannot go on any further"*. The LORD wasted no time in starting our romance and showing me His great love for me. He has wooed me like no other suitor I have ever known. He sends me falling stars, butterfly kisses and even writes love notes to me in the sky. Who needs jewels around their neck when I can gaze up into a dark night sky full of sparkling diamonds whenever I want? He sends birds to sing me awake each morning and paints me masterpieces in the sky every evening at sunset. Over the past three years because of His romantic pursuit to mend my broken heart *I have fallen hopelessly in love with Jesus forever*! He is my knight in shining armor who rescued me from the tower of darkness and pain I lived in most of my life and now I never want to be separated from His presence again. I am a child of the **"Most High God"** and princess bride of the **"King of Kings"** and **I will live happily forever after!**

Listen to these beautiful words from my 'Prince Charming', He is calling your name—can you hear His sweet voice? Fall into His arms and let him sweep you away because **He thinks you are beautiful!**

> *"My lover spoke and said to me, 'Arise, my darling, my beautiful one, and come with me. See! The winter is past; the rains are over and gone. Flowers appear on the earth; the season of singing has come, the cooing of doves is heard in our land. The fig tree forms its early fruit; the blossoming vines spread their fragrance. Arise, come, my darling; my beautiful one, come with me."*
> Song of Songs 2:10-13

Chapter 12

The Journey Home

On many days during the writing of this book about my long journey back home to my precious 'Abba' Father, I listened to a ***truly beautiful song*** whose words I want to share with you below. It sings so completely my own personal journey home that was filled with such desperate pain most of the way. Oh precious one, the deep love, joy and peace I have finally found is truly indescribable and was worth every painful step in my search for my 'Prince'! Listen closely; hear the melody and Jesus' sweet voice, **HE'S SINGING YOU HOME!**

"THE JOURNEY HOME"

*"The journey home
Is never too long
Your heart arrives before the train
The journey home
Is never too long
Some yesterdays always remain*

*I'm going back to where my heart was light
When my pillow was a ship I sailed through the night*

*The journey home is never too long
When open arms are waiting there
The journey home is never too long
There's room to love and room to spare*

*I want to feel the way that I did there
And think my wishes through before I wish again*

*The journey home is never too long
Home hopes to heal the deepest pain
The journey home is never too long
Your heart arrives before the train*

*Not every boat you come across is one you have to take
Now sometimes 'standing still' can be the best move you ever make."*[6]

Oh precious one, the journey home is worth the trip! My prayer for you today is that my words will cause you to hear His voice and seek His love for yourselves. **RUN**, with all your might, to the **well filled with 'living waters'**! Can you see Him—He's standing there by the well with open arms waiting for you! He longs to quench your thirst forever! Please don't miss the abundant life filled with overflowing waters of love, joy, and peace that Jesus died to give you. The cost to you—is **free**, Jesus has already paid the ultimate price—***His life in exchange for yours***. Drink long and deep from the 'living water' and live!

For in HIM is life! (John 1:4)

"They said to the woman, 'We no longer believe just because of what you said; now we have heard for ourselves, and we know that this man really is the Savior of the world." (John 4:42)

A Prayer for Salvation

If, while you have been reading this book, you have realized you are not sure that you really know this 'Prince of Peace' named Jesus then please let me share a prayer below that will open the door for your romance with Him to begin. If you pray this prayer I promise you your life will never be the same! Don't be discouraged in the beginning, it will take time, just like it has with me, for you to grow in your relationship with Him—but *oh how wonderful your journey will be*! If you don't own a Bible then buy one **immediately** and **started reading** *His love letter to you*, it will be the road map for your new journey. That is how you will grow in your knowledge of Him. He will never leave you nor forsake you and when at times you get tired, He will carry you when you can't walk any further. He will help you to know the love of the Father and they will love you **forever with an everlasting love! Pray these words from your heart:**

Dear Heavenly Father,

I acknowledge to You that I am a sinner and cannot save myself. I believe that your Son Jesus Christ died on the cross in my place for my sins and rose from the dead to give me salvation. I now accept the Lord Jesus Christ as my personal Savior, trusting Him alone to give me eternal life and a relationship with You. I give every part of my life totally to You. Thank You for saving me, and help me from this day on to live a life that is pleasing to You. Amen.

Congratulations and welcome to the Family of God!

"The Spirit and the bride say, 'Come!' And let him who hears say, 'Come!' Whoever is thirsty, let him come; and whoever wishes, let him take the free gift of the water of life."

Revelation 22:17

About the Author

Tassy Wofford is the mother of one daughter, two cats and a **crazy** African gray parrot. She lives with her cats and parrot in Florence, South Carolina. Along with being the author of this book Tassy is an accomplished artist and also created the painting for the cover of her book. She is most well known for her realistic portraits of children, adults and pets. Many of her portraits hang in private homes, colleges and hospitals across the United States. The place she is **most honored** to have one of her portraits hanging is in the **Ronald Reagan Library**. Her 'big dream' for her art is to one day have one of her portraits hanging permanently in the greatest home in the land, **The White House**. Her **greatest passion** in life now is to see others 'set free' from emotional pain and receive the healing Jesus died to give.

If you would like to share with Tassy any encouragement or hope you received while reading her story, *"I Was the Woman at the Well"* please feel free to email your comments to her at tassyart@bellsouth.net.

Notes

[1] (Aramaic word for "Daddy or "Papa")

[2] Ralph Gower, "The New Manners & Customs of Bible Times, "(Moody Press of Chicago, Illinois. Copyright The Moody Bible Institute, © 1987 and 2000) p. 28.

[3] Webster's *The New American Webster Handy College Dictionary*, New 3rd ed. (New York/NY: Penguin Books USA, 1995) n. "well," "issue."

[4] Webster's *The New American Webster Handy College Dictionary*, New 3rd ed. (New York/NY: Penguin Books USA, 1995) v.i. "issue."

[5] Webster's *The New American Webster Handy College Dictionary*, New 3rd ed. (New York/NY: Penguin Books USA, 1995) n., v.t., "promise"

[6] "The Journey Home", "Harem", Sarah Brightman, Angel Records, NY, 2003, Music & Lyrics by A. R. Rahman & Don Black

Printed in the United States
98455LV00002B/118/A